Strai  Anthology
Volume 1

Strangest Fiction Publishing

Orchestrated and Judged by Derek Wautlet and Josh Spicer
Cover Art by Brendan Walfield

ISBN: 9798355543303

DEDICATION

This book is dedicated to all the wonderful writers that have contributed to strangestfiction.com and helped it blossom into the community it is today!

CONTENTS

FOREWORD

The true meaning of "strange fiction" in our sense of the word is hard to define concretely. More than anything it is a feeling you get when a piece of fiction is dark, unsettling, twisted, or paranormal. It is a feeling that lives in the chill that crawls its way down your spine when you read a particularly unsettling passage. It lives in your curiosity, obsession even, with a dark alternate universe that an author has created before your very eyes. It lives in your disbelief with the thought of brother fighting brother in the most brutal way possible. It lives in the heart pounding quest that the author has sent you on with a few mythical companions and a sword forged of immortal steel.

Strange fiction has always been the genre I've loved to create in, ever since I was a child. Back then I wasn't writing down my ideas, though, I was imagining them. I would conjure up strange worlds in my mind with fearless protagonists and a never ending supply of new quests. I wouldn't need to write down my ideas or share them with any sort of audience. I was *living* the adventure and that was enough for me. As I grew and my writing matured, a desire grew to share my writing with others and give them the keys to the worlds I had created.

This incessant need to put my work out there ultimately came to a head a year and a half ago in Spring 2021. I always wanted to share my own writing with the world but also knew how valuable a community could be. I had seen friends and colleagues waiting months for responses from flaky literary journals. I wanted to bring a place where we could create our "strange" fiction together and help each other grow. I had thought about creating a Wattpad copycat, or another sort of literary application with more mass appeal. Ultimately, though, I knew the genre I really wanted to write in, and I had a suspicion that other writers out there would be interested in the same. Those that wander into a bookstore feeling cornered into one particular subset of fiction but are feeling that their interests don't fall so neatly into one aisle. Those that crave the supernatural, science fiction, horror, and more all at once. I then started work on this hub for strange fiction and after many late night coding sessions, strangestfiction.com was born.

Over the past year we've seen excellent growth and attracted just the right group of talented strange fiction writers we were hoping for. I am beyond thrilled to be introducing our first ever anthology: Strangest Fiction Anthology - Volume 1. For this collection of short stories, we brought together eighteen of the most popular stories from our site, strangestfiction.com, to be featured in a reader friendly format.

We judged many stories, but the ones that we chose were ones that made us emote. Made us stop and think. Made us feel. We wanted stories that we would remember and talk about constantly. The stories we selected for inclusion affected us in these ways. We wanted stories that fit with our mission to create stories that overflow with a creativity that manifests in the world of the strange. In this anthology, we want to display that creativity and show off the community we have created. A community that is chalk full of writers that come from all over the world, and are eclectic in character. They all have one thing in common; a love for writing. A passion for putting pen to paper in the most creative ways possible. This is the product of blood, sweat and tears of writers who are passionate about what they do. Here you go, reader; read their words and travel to worlds built by strange minds.

Happy reading,

Derek Wautlet

Founder of strangestfiction.com

UPSTAIRS
By Jon Richter

"I heard it again today," she said cautiously.

Chris nodded his agreement, eyes still fixed on the screen. He did this a lot, accompanied by a sort of wide-eyed, enthusiastic 'mmm' sound, which meant he hadn't listened to a word she'd said.

"Chris, I think there's something living up there."

No response this time, except for a muttered curse as a speculative long shot sailed over the crossbar.

"Will you go up and have a look?"

That one seemed to register, and he turned to look at her, suddenly exasperated.

"Sandy, I'm watching the bloody football. Can't you go and do it?"

She shrugged, eyes cast downwards. "I would… I'm just a bit scared." She knew this was a cheap tactic. But he was always more compliant when she was playing the part of a damsel in distress. When they had met, she had been very young. It was just the way their relationship worked.

He rolled his eyes. "Alright, alright. I'll go up there at halftime. It's probably just a squirrel or something. We'll need to buy some traps."

A part of her instinctively wanted to say, 'oh no, please don't kill it,' but in truth, she didn't mind at all if he did. The noise had been driving her crazy. Every day, while Chris was at the factory, she was trying to get some work done in the study. The intermittent sound of movement directly above her as she sat at her desk.

Something in the attic.

She'd lived with mice before, in a shared house as a student, and was familiar with the scratching, scrambling sound as they scuttled along rafters and floorboards and chewed everything in sight. This sound was different. Heavier, almost like footfalls – but not feet, exactly. More of a slapping noise, almost like... *hands*. Trying to block it out of her mind only seemed to summon ever more ludicrous or disturbing visions of what might be crawling around upstairs.

An escaped criminal... a deformed child... a humanoid monster, padding around the loft on all fours, but upside down, its arms and legs bent sickeningly backward.

She was a literary agent, one of the few that specialized in horror fiction, and she knew her daily immersion in terrifying manuscripts (the good ones, at least) was probably not helping. In recent days she had become so tense that she was unable to concentrate on work at all – she just sat there, nerves stretched taut as tripwires, awaiting with dread the next inevitable snatch of sound from above. And her mind began to play other tricks on her. Now it wasn't just the weird flap-flapping footsteps she could hear; there was also breathing, perhaps even a sniffing sound, as the intruder investigated its surroundings like some hideous blind cave monster.

Sandy tried to pay attention to the match and forget about it. Half time arrived with the game still goalless, and with a sigh, Chris hauled himself up from the sofa and trudged wearily up the stairs. She heard the sound of the loft hatch opening, the ladder being pulled down and fixed in place, and metallic clangs as her husband began to ascend.

Chris was a good, simple man. He knew all of her foibles, her little obsessions, the many layers of her self-doubt. He grumbled and complained and resented her 'easy life' of home-working, but ultimately he understood, he tolerated, he supported her in his own quiet way. He just… *was*. With Chris, she felt safe, comfortable. He held her down to earth like a tight grip on a balloon string.

When the second set of adverts finished and the players started to line up for the second half, she realized he had been up there for fifteen minutes. As she rose and called his name, she heard the sound of his footfalls on the ladder once again.

He didn't reply. She heard the ladder sliding back up into the loft, the hatch closing, and his footsteps coming down the stairs. He headed straight into the kitchen and switched on the kettle.

"Well? Did you find anything?" she called after him, irritated.

There was only the sound of the boiling water and the tinkling of a teaspoon against the sides of a mug.

"Chris? Was there anything up there?" she insisted, striding into the kitchen.

He turned to face her, and smiled.

"Nope. Couldn't see anything. Sorry love. Do you want a

cuppa?"

"Really? There weren't any… droppings or anything like that? Was all our stuff okay?"

Chris shrugged.

"Sorry, Sandy. It's just the attic. I shone my torch around a bit, looked all over, but couldn't see anything funny. Are you sure you're definitely not just hearing pigeons on the roof, maybe?"

She wanted to shout at him, wanted to tell him he hadn't looked properly. Go and grab the torch and pull down the ladder and head up there herself, show him what a sloppy job he had done. *If you want something done properly, do it yourself,* as her mother always said. He was always so bloody laid back.

But, even though she'd been up into the loft many times before, searching for cookbooks or misplaced old contact numbers or the spare iron when the main one had broken, she suddenly realized that she couldn't go up there anymore. She was frightened. Chris's failure to find *whatever it was* only meant that it was clever, that it knew how to hide. A crouching tangle of limbs, compressed into a dark corner, a pair of slitted crimson eyes watching as her husband ineptly wafted the torch around.

"Never mind," she muttered. "I'm going to bed. Enjoy the rest of the match." But he hadn't heard her, because Spurs had scored, and he was already dashing into the front room to celebrate like a happy child.

***

She stared into the monitor, eyes feeling as though someone had injected lead into them. She had barely slept. Her ears, her brain, had been too alive, listening intently for sounds from above. At one point, she thought she'd heard the eerie slapping footfalls scurrying across the attic floor… but perhaps she'd nodded off and dreamt it. Chris, of course, was sound asleep throughout, content after his beloved team's victory and his three celebratory cans of Guinness.

The next morning she was already sitting at the computer sipping coffee when he awoke.

"Bloody hell, Sandy; did you wet the bed?"

She knew she must look a state – she was still wearing her dressing gown and hadn't even showered.

"No, I just need to get an early start on some work."

"Alright. Well, I'd better get to work myself." He shut himself in the bathroom, and she could hear the sounds of running water and the electric toothbrush.

Nothing from upstairs.

Chris went to work, and Sandy tried to plow through some manuscripts, mediocre submissions from new writers who she let down as gently as she could. She had never felt so utterly on edge. Each tiny sound – a knocking pipe, a birdcall outside the window, a passing car – almost sent her into a state of frenzy.

But still, complete silence from her unwanted guest. Was it taunting her? Was this its revenge against her for dispatching someone to investigate its lair?

Get a grip, Sandy!

The day seemed endless, and when Chris finally returned, she almost broke down in tears as she hugged him. Even her husband, who at times had the empathy of a house brick, sensed that she was fragile, and upset. Instead of bemoaning his long hard day, he went into the kitchen and began the ritual of cooking their tea, a rare occurrence that would utilize around three times as many pans and plates as were actually needed and was usually reserved for when he had done something wrong. Maybe he thought he had. She knew she was being irrational, hysterical, pathetic.

She drank an entire bottle of wine with the fish dish he prepared and, this time, managed to fall into a deep sleep.

***

The next morning she stayed in bed late. Chris seemed amused as he kissed her goodbye. He was being remarkably nice this week, a part of her brain observed. But the rest of her mind was already moving on to the attic, which remained disconcertingly quiet.

She pictured the thing, crouching in the shadows, perfectly still. Lurking. Smiling.

She showered, dressed, and ate breakfast. It was midday by the time she sat at her computer. Still, she hadn't heard a sound from above. She switched the computer on, began opening e-mails, and tried to focus. A manuscript held her attention briefly, but after a while, she found she was reading whole paragraphs without taking in a single word. Something about an elderly couple and euthanasia. The sort of stuff that might move her to tears if written well. But once again, she couldn't concentrate on it. This was getting ridiculous.

With a horrible feeling of dread that seemed to radiate out from her stomach, she realized that she would have to go and look around up there to see for herself.

She wouldn't tell Chris she'd done it. She would just take a deep breath, climb the ladder quickly, and shine the torch in a 360-degree rotation. Surprise the creature before it could scamper back into its hiding place.

She walked into the hallway and stared up at the loft's access hatch, shrinking from it a little as if she expected it to suddenly yawn open and expel some leering horror down upon her. Her eyes shifted to the nearby storage cupboard, a strange little walk-in space where they kept an assortment of junk. Their house wasn't big enough for a garage or even a garden shed, and so Chris had to keep his tools in there.

Sandy opened the cupboard and took out the toolbox. Rifling through its contents, she eventually settled on the hammer and took a practice swing at the head of an imaginary beast in the hallway. It felt unwieldy, inaccurate. She wondered if maybe a kitchen knife would serve her better. Or maybe one of the other tools in the cupboard. She put the hammer on the ground and rummaged again inside the storeroom, wondering if the thing could hear her, if it knew she was trying to select the best weapon with which to bludgeon it to death.

Or simply to fend it off.

In the end, she remembered Chris's snooker cue, shoved under their bed with various other sporting paraphernalia from his various 'phases' (it was collecting dust alongside a badminton racket, a hockey stick, and an American football). It was a gift from his brother, who had jokingly inscribed it with the name 'The Shaft,' and unscrewed it into two parts. The base was light enough for her to swing properly but heavy enough to still feel dangerous.

She returned to the landing, clutching her new cudgel, looking up once again at the innocuous rectangle of the access hatch. Still, she felt underprepared, exposed. Rats might scurry up her legs beneath the skirt she was wearing. Something clinging to the ceiling might drop and claw at her eyes. She needed more protection.

She went back into the bedroom and opened the wardrobe that contained Chris's clothes. She put on his tracksuit pants, and zipped his high-vis running jacket over her blouse. Then she went to find her wellies and put them on, tucking the tracksuit pants into them.

Another flash of inspiration. She crouched to search under the bed once again, this time for the bag full of fancy dress costumes from parties they had been to. She found it (thank god it hadn't been stored in the loft) and took out a rubber skull mask that Chris had once worn to a Hallowe'en party. Sandy had been Morticia

Addams, as she recalled, and had really wanted him to go as Gomez, but for some reason, he'd been really keen on this stupid mask and an accompanying black morph suit with a glow-in-the-dark skeleton on it.

That had been... god, nearly five years ago. She looked in the mirror at her gaudy ensemble. She'd put on so much weight since then. Really *aged*. She sighed and put on the mask.

Visibility wasn't great from underneath it, but she did feel better, shielded, as though she had donned a ridiculous suit of armor. The skull grinned back at her from the mirror, eyeless sockets gaping. *The only monster in this house is you, Sandy.* She gripped the snooker cue like a truncheon and stepped out onto the landing once again. She found the long pole in the storage cupboard that enabled her to open the loft hatch and unhook the ladder, which retracted at the top. The dark oblong above was like a window into another world, a black void, like part of a computer game that you weren't supposed to access, where they hadn't programmed in any background texture. That reminded her to pick up the torch once again from inside the cupboard. The darkness seemed so absolute that she almost expected it to consume the flashlight's beam, but instead, it illuminated the dusty, cobwebbed ceiling above, and she began to ascend, having to grip the sides of the ladder while still holding on to the torch and the snooker cue.

Her whole body tensed as she ascended each step, trying to do it quickly, not to think about what she was doing, what she would find up there. About those weird, slapping footfalls. She imagined something waiting for her, perched like a gargoyle just beyond the lip of the entrance hatch.

Then the front door opened downstairs.

"Hiya, Sandy! I'm home early!"

She stopped, breathless, trembling. What would Chris think of her, halfway up the ladder, frozen in terror, dressed like a lunatic?

Better she carried on, finished the job. If she did see something, at least he was here now to help her. She wondered why he was home so early from work.

Grimly, she continued her climb. Her head was above the ceiling, inside the attic. She could smell the expected musty odor, but also something else, like the sickly sweet smell of an overflowing bin, in summer. She raised the torch.

She saw the familiar boxes and bags that had been 'temporarily' stored up there years ago. The breeze-block walls, more cobwebs, the wooden flooring. The painting they had bought on holiday was still propped against the wall, never quite fitting with the rest of their decor.

The torchlight panned across the scene. There was no movement, no sound at all, except for Chris calling to her from downstairs.

She turned around.

She gasped.

The bricks behind her were covered with some sort of thick webbing. Milky-white strands crisscrossed the wall, plaited together like ropes. It was as though a million spiders had made a home of the entire back portion of the loft.

Or one gigantic one.

Shaking, she moved her torch across the glistening mass. At one point, it bulged outwards as though concealing something. At the top of the swelling, something protruded from the web (for she had begun to think of it as such now, a single enormous web, the source of the terrible noise, some aberration that had moved into their attic and had been torturing her for weeks – how had Chris not noticed this when he went up there?). She stepped gingerly closer, trying to make sense of it.

It was a pair of feet.

There was a body hanging there, upside down, encased in the threads of this vile nest.

"Sandy?" came the voice, now from the bottom of the stairs. "Where are you?"

She tried to call out to him, but her vocal cords were frozen, her mouth open in the shape of a soundless scream. The torch beam shook as it moved downwards, over the bulge that she now knew was the shape of a human body, towards the face that hung out of the other end, inches above the floor.

An eyeless face to match her skull mask. A dark puddle below it where blood had trickled from its gouged sockets. The mouth contorted into a terrible expression but instantly familiar.

It was Chris.

The torch clattered to the floor, the beam pointing away from the grotesque tableau.

She heard footsteps coming up the stairs, a final cry of, "Sandy?"

Then a pause, followed by a long, disappointed sigh. And finally, a strange hissing sound, like the air being let out of an inflatable.

Then silence.

She bent to pick up the torch, her mind feeling as though it was about to break.

If Chris was… then what…

She heard the slapping sound then, the sound like the footfalls of something that were not feet, on the floor of the landing below.

At that point, she finally screamed, just as the sounds reached the ladder, and the thing that was not her husband began to climb.

She stumbled backward, falling over one of the boxes. This time it was the snooker cue that fell from her grasp, rolling away into the darkness. All she had was the torch, aimed at the hatch, waiting for something to emerge, something that had killed her husband and… *replaced* him.

Another step on the ladder… another…

Sandy ducked behind a pile of boxes, whimpering.

Then the loft hatch slammed closed, and all she heard was the sound of hammering.

THE WORDBRAND
By Titania Tempest

Embry…

The whispering, like wind caressing parchment, curled out from the depths of the library. Even though she was expecting it, Embry jumped violently at the sound of her name and knocked a teetering stack of books to rocking at the edge of her writing desk. With a muffled curse, she whipped out a deft hand to steady them and then sat perfectly still, listening hard to gauge the direction of the call.

Embry.

It came again, a hollow echo twisting amongst the laden shelves. A soft rasp, rustling, ancient…. impossible. Embry pursed her lips; subconsciously, she rested her left hand upon the hilt of her blade, thumbing the dent in the pommel. It wasn't the first time she had heard the scratchy whispers, but it had been a long time—and she had half-heartedly hoped she wouldn't ever again.

She had hoped that she was well past the dreadful phenomenon, that it was just an unpleasant, distant memory. Unwilling to respond, she fiddled with her short sword for a moment more.

EMBRY!

With a huff, she pushed to her feet. Light as a cat, she skirted several large shelves and headed towards the shadowed recesses at the back of the library. It was darker here, a windowless labyrinth of tomes secreted away from any hope of moonlight. Here and there, breaking the monotony of hundreds of shelves, false torches flickered, adding to the heavy, antiquated ambiance.

Embry inhaled deeply, breathing in the dusty scent of ancient pages—pages thumbed by thousands of hands, holding silent testimony to thousands of unspoken stories. As she flitted deeper into the recesses of knowledge, she ran her finger along the edges of misshapen old spines, relishing the feel of leather and fabric. Reverent, she let her fingers linger over each, even as she quickened her pace. She used to love coming to the library, but she had been avoiding it for a long, long time—ever since the whispers had become so frequent, she couldn't sleep.

Unfortunately, one can only forestall fate for so long before it catches up... And caught her it had.

She slowed as she turned into the aisle second from last, a corridor flanked by row upon row of huge, brooding tomes. She felt the air change, frosty, brittle, and laced through with a hint of desperation. Unerringly, her feet carried her to a book on the third-from-bottom shelf, a smaller volume flanked by unforgiving giants. Embry blew her hair out of her eyes, steeled herself, and reached for it before she could change her mind.

The inky velvet cover burned beneath her touch, and she gritted her teeth against the familiar insistent rush of spirit. Holding it firmly with both hands, she sank down with her legs folded and cradled it in her lap. For a long moment, she simply stared down at it.

Embry…!

"All right," she grumbled. "Gods, give me a break."

She opened the small black book to a random page roughly halfway through. The text was neat and ordered, the absolute opposite of the chaos she knew she was about to experience. Clasping it carefully in one hand, she drew back the other and then, before she could indulge her faintness of heart, plunged her palm down to slam flat against the coarse parchment.

At once, three hundred years of history crashed mercilessly through her mind; laughing families, cooing lovers, desperate fathers, poverty, hope, heartache, and everything in between. The echo of the writer's spirit encased within the pages dragged her conscious along in a relentless vice-grip at a pace over which she had no control. With unstoppable rapidity, she approached the line of light she now knew denoted the jump from past to future.

She hit it hard. The searing brightness was blinding, insufferable, and she screamed with the effort of not clawing out her own eyes as she hurtled across the breach.

On the other side, darkness engulfed her; the fog of the unknown, of that which should not be known—but which the spirits of writers long dead forced upon her.

After a tense moment, the shadow of nothingness cleared to reveal a blonde girl, no more than twenty-four, vibrant and laughing.

A flicker and the joy was gone; the pretty face contorted with panic at being ensnared when she least expected it. She was pinned beneath a shadowed man with ice-blue eyes, a man with a lopsided smile that might have been impish on a child but was terrifying on the visage of a killer.

The girl's mouth was frozen open in a silent scream as she desperately scrabbled to fend off her demise.

A hatchet split her skull, spilling her physical thoughts into the man's large, sensitive hands. Her eyes bulged, dislodged by the force of the blow, and her slack mouth lost the will of its scream. The man tinkered lovingly with the gray matter that should have been hidden away on the inside of her head; he reveled in it in the helplessness of his victim, and Embry swirled on a rising tide of nausea.

But the spirit pulled her back, tumbling her in rewind through the ghosts of the vision. Unceremoniously, it spat her back into the present, and then she was simply rocking in place over a harmless book, crying and shaking and swallowing bile. Revolted, she flung the offending object as far as she could and drew her knees up, wrapping her arms around them and burying her face to stem the tears.

That was, without a doubt, the most horrific one yet. And it was exactly the reason she hated her "gift."

Around her, a soft, sullen breeze fitted, rustling non-existent pages, tugging at her long titian hair and pressing for her answer.

But the violent murder replayed in her mind, again and again, and she defied the insistent whispering as long as she could stand. She had no desire—no desire whatsoever—to get involved with what she had just seen.

The whispers gained momentum, incessant, a clamoring hiss rising on a tide of objection at her lack of response. At last, Embry sat up, angrily pushing tears from her lashes, and forced herself to her feet. Really, it was a miracle no one else in the world could hear them. She drew the Written Blade, which whispered in its own way—silently, by means of scrawling scripts that fade and ink across the silver surface of its cutting edge. Resigned to her fate, as usual, she sighed as she traipsed the length of the corridor.

She bent down and picked up the book.

The whispers stilled as she dusted off the cover, and an expectant silence reigned. A thousand unseen eyes, the forgotten remnants of history, watched her with solemn intensity.

Embry held the book aloft and touched the tip of the Written Blade to its velvet cover. She opened her awareness willingly to meet the spirit echo of its author.

"When?" she asked.

The answer was instantaneous as if the essence all but exploded with its request.

Now-now-now-now...!

"Where?"

Go-now-go-now-go-now!

Embry lowered the book and narrowed her eyes. She sheathed her blade and then folded her arms around the tome. "You can write an entire novel, but you can't find the words to tell me where I must go to save your imperiled descendant?"

An abashed shuffling answered her, a page equivalent of throat-clearing. The dusty rasp came again, clearer, less hurried, careful to make its point known.

Alcott... Alehouse.

Embry nodded her understanding but scoffed at the ancient colloquialism. "We call it a nightclub nowadays."

Unseen vestiges bridled at her insolence, but she ignored them. Carefully, she slid the book back into its allotted space between the two imposing volumes that guarded it. Softly, she stroked one finger against the spine, a featherlight promise pressed into gold lettering. Her other hand thumbed the dent in the pommel of the Written Blade.

She tilted her head sideways to read the author's mark. "Alice... Deveray... Very well. I will find your descendant, Alice, and I will prevent her fate. This I swear to you."

A roar of air engulfed her, and Embry smiled despite herself. If she'd never felt a spirit hug her before, she was sure she had now. That, and that alone, convinced her she had made the right decision in coming down to the library tonight.

Firmly, she nodded, and the whisperings sputtered into nothingness. Embry straightened her jacket and brushed away silver motes of ancient dust, the flakes of magic seeped free from stories over eons. Pulling up her collar, she turned her back on the dusky aisle and strode directly into fate's focus.

As she stepped clear of the library, a wave of fresh, brittle air engulfed her. Despite the thick mantle of the night around her, she could smell the sea not far away, all seaweed and brine and mystery. The library door clicked quietly closed behind her, locked as it had been when she arrived. Without sparing a glance for the phenomenon, she pulled a cigarette out of her jacket pocket and ignited it, drawing sharply on the astringent menthol. She exhaled blue smoke, leaving it hanging in a hazy cloud beneath the lamp that illuminated the library stairs.

Elegant as a dancer, wary as a fox, she descended and crossed the street. Alcott's wasn't far away; it sprawled along the edge of the nearby harbor, all lights, and alcohol and allure.

Embry's least favorite kind of place. She could hear the throbbing music from here.

Another drag of her cigarette, two more streets, and then she stood at the far end of its car park opposite garish doors, staring at the seething mass of bodies within. Flashing strobes leaked spears of light into the dark sky, disturbing the unbroken horizon of the night with chaotic swirls that leaped in time to a heavy baseline. Embry's mouth tightened with disapproval. Why people couldn't just sit quietly and listen to the sounds of life was beyond her. This incessant need to chase libations, loose dreams, and hazy memories was a mystery she would never understand.

And she understood some unusual mysteries.

She perked up when she caught sight of the blonde, though. There was no doubt whatsoever that she was the same girl from the vision. Embry took another drag of her cigarette, but her fingers crumpled it as the girl's dance partner turned in her direction. Her left hand traveled unerringly to the hilt of her blade.

The man with the ice-blue eyes.

Even from her vantage, Embry could see his soul was broken. She stifled a shiver of disgust, glaring at him like a cat that's spotted a snake. And the girl... naïve, lively, unaware of the devil she danced with. Embry suddenly realized she was smoking her bent filter and crushed out the remains of her cigarette against the tarmac before lighting another. Her nerves flickered as she held the lighter steady, but her eyes remained fixed and unwavering, set upon the charming psychopath.

He moved energetically, his form athletic and strong. Predatory. His soulless eyes drank the girl in, spinning her into his arms and out again until she was giddy with music and drunk on dancing. Her face glowed, full of irresistible life, and Embry decided it was her very liveliness that had lured him to her to begin with. She was electric—afire with the joy of existence. Her hips swayed with effortless grace, swirling her across the dancefloor in mesmerizing patterns. She had a beautiful smile, open and trusting, and sparkling eyes of rich hazel that contrasted magnificently with her platinum hair. She was destined to be a martyr of beauty, a creature cursed to discover the potential truth of its dark worth...

Unless Embry interfered.

By the end of Embry's third cigarette, the mismatched couple had relinquished the dancefloor. Breathless, laughing, they stopped for another drink and then strolled, arm in arm, out towards the wharf. Flitting through the shadows, Embry followed, ever the watcher in the night.

At the far end of the pier, the pair clambered playfully onto a small yacht and shared a "Titanic" moment at the point of the prow. Embry's jaw tightened to watch the spider spin his web with such frightening precision. The girl was oblivious to the beast singing her into range. They tumbled into a giggling heap on the forward deck, and Embry alighted on the stern unnoticed. Deftly, she freed the Written Blade from its sheath, curling her long fingers around the staghorn hilt and thumbing the familiar dent in the pommel as she settled it in her hand.

She knew what had happened next, and she was ready.

Ducking under the boom, she crouched in the shadow of the mast and waited. Below her, mischievous wrestling suddenly turned to true struggle, and the girl cried out in pain. She fought him like a wildcat, but he was too strong.

Trapping her with one powerful arm, he reached across with the other for the fireman's axe kept aboard for emergencies. The girl's eyes followed the movement and registered panic. She kicked and bucked, clawing at his face, arms, chest—anything she could reach—but he held her fast, pinned down by that feral smile. He reared up above her, crushing her with his weight, keeping her trapped as he hefted the axe.

Embry launched herself into the night air, raining down upon him like hellfire. She wasted no time on warning, on idle threats, nor on the possibility of his repentance at being caught in the act. He was guilty; she had seen it. She had no doubt, also, by the effortless way he manhandled the girl, that she was not his first.

She was simply the first that had words in her blood, a writer in her ancestry, an echo spirit to prompt rescue in her direction.

Luckily for her, the books had spoken on her behalf.

And—luckier for her—the Wordbrand had chosen to listen.

Embry collided with her target with all the force of a hurricane, burying the dagger hilt-deep into the vulnerable flesh of his neck. The blade hissed, the words on its surface white-hot and scudding in and out of visibility like lightning. Both the man and the girl froze in surprise, their gazes molded to Embry's winter visage. The man sputtered; the vulgar enthusiasm in his ice-blue eyes extinguished in the face of his own mortality. Embry thumbed the pommel again, set her stance, and then, with slow malice, carved the blade sideways to sever his jugular.

Blood gushed, spraying across the girl, who screamed and raised her arms to shield her face from the crimson deluge. The man toppled sideways off her, sliding free of the sword and gurgling wet attempts at breath as he crumpled. He clutched at his slashed throat, trying to stem a tsunami with his fingers, and stared hatefully up at Embry. He seemed unable to comprehend his own demise, holding onto denial until the last.

But finally, he stilled. His ice-blue eyes, wide and glassy, stared into nothing. One hand dangled limply at his throat, useless. Dark rivulets of blood pooled beneath his shaggy head, questing out across the deck of the yacht, and Embry spat down onto his prostrate corpse. She plucked up his discarded shirt and used it to wipe the wicked blade of her sword until not a spot of his blood defiled it.

Sliding the Written Blade back into its sheath, Embry turned to the girl, who cowered hunched against a lifering.

"Are you Hale?" Embry asked. She looked down at the girl with mild curiosity—a fragile thing, this close.

"Who"—the girl swallowed—"who are you?" The words were hardly a squeak, pushed unsteadily out from a throat constricted by fear.

Embry thumbed the pommel again, heard the whisper, and raised an eyebrow.

"Does the name Alice Deveray mean anything to you?"

The girl blinked. She stared up at Embry for a long moment as if trying to understand the question. At last, she gave a hesitant nod.

"My great-great-grandmother…"

Embry nodded. Of course she was. That was how it worked.

"She sends her regards."

She turned to leave, but the girl shifted abruptly.

"Wait! I… um—thank you… for…" She broke off, her frightened gaze flickering briefly to the still form of her would-be murderer. "C-can I repay you, somehow?"

Embry paused, considering. Absentmindedly, she checked that the Written Blade was secure in its scabbard and then tilted her head.

"Make a donation to your local library. Tell them it's on behalf of the Wordbrand."

Beset by confusion, the girl opened her mouth to respond, but Embry was gone.

Silent as a wraith, quick as a shadow—gone.

And the girl was left behind, blood-soaked but unharmed; alone but for the corpse of an ice-eyed man. Alone, but alive. Just as Embry promised.

SUMMER STORM
By Steve DeGroof

Tatiana lay on the floor, drawing her pictures. Scattered around her were crayons and sheets of paper. Real crayons and real paper, mind you. Nothing but the best for their little girl. They'd tried to get her to use a tablet, but she insisted on crayons and paper, so that's what they gave her.

After all, she was a celebrity – the celebrity. The most famous person on the planet. Irene and Paul had gone to great lengths to ensure Tatiana would be the first child born on Demeter.

It started with arranging to be on the first Hermes colony ship. Then, they made sure that they'd be revived early from stasis. Ten percent of all colonists were taken out of stasis a year before arrival, mainly for planning and preparation, but also because the last thing you want is your entire population landing on a new planet, all suffering from stasis hangovers at once.

During that year, they worked out the logistics of Irene's pregnancy. They weren't the only ones shooting for having the first baby born on Demeter, of course. The first human born on any extrasolar planet? Huge deal. And they'd beat all the competition. Irene went into labor while Hermes 1 was entering Demeter's atmosphere and gave birth right there on the landing pad.

The First Demeterian! The Miracle Baby!

To be fair, there was nothing particularly miraculous about it unless you consider a big old shot of oxytocin to be a miracle.

They'd paid a lot of money and timed it just right. You know what they say, you have to spend money to make money. And they definitely made money out of the deal.

Tatiana-branded merchandise practically sold itself. And the drawings she made with her precious crayons and paper, Irene and Paul could sell those for up to five hundred a pop. The girl was really talented. But five hundred for a crayon drawing? Let's face it, her celebrity counted for a good percentage of that price.

Not that they were complaining or anything. The merch and the drawings paid the bills, and then some. And, with every colony ship that arrived, there was a new batch of customers eager to hand over their hard-earned cash. Tatiana had already built up a sizable trust fund and was only six years old.

Irene and Paul made sure they kept digital copies of all Tatiana's artwork. It really was amazing. Paul watched her work, blending the colors with her thumb, making each line and contour just so. If it weren't for the fact that they were made from wax on paper, you'd swear they were photographs.

All her drawings were landscapes of Demeter, each one amazingly beautiful. Demeter itself was amazingly beautiful. And it looked a lot like Earth. Well, a lot like Earth did before humans poisoned it and paved it over.

The Demeter colonists were trying to do better this time. Keeping things as green as possible. And Demeter was definitely green. The first settlement, Eleusis, where Paul and Irene lived, was nestled between the Pax Ocean and the Verde Mountains.

Gentle ocean breezes, amazing sunsets, and some of the best planting soil ever. The seeds the colonists had brought from Earth sprouted immediately and grew like weeds. Eleusis had more than enough to eat and plenty of feed for the livestock they'd brought with them in stasis.

Eleusis was primarily an agricultural settlement, with a lot of high tech discreetly tucked away, out of sight. If you didn't look at the electric tractors too closely, you'd miss that there wasn't anyone driving them. Oh, there were plenty of maintenance and service robots around, but they were kept out of sight when not in use. Wouldn't want to ruin the illusion, after all.

Demeter wasn't the first extrasolar planet targeted for colonization. Far from it. There were at least a hundred other Earth-like planets currently being terraformed by armies of robots. The thing was, Demeter came ready-made for human settlement. You could've plopped a person down just about anywhere on the surface, armed with nothing more than a pocket knife, and they would've been able to survive without much trouble.

The planet was amazing. Never mind the near-perfect nitrogen/oxygen atmospheric mix or the surface gravity that was 99% Earth normal. Most of its land surface was covered in forests, marshes, and grassland, and almost every plant had something on it that was edible. The fruit of the peach apple tree, for example, makes the best pie filling or, if you're so inclined, the best cider.

And it wasn't just the native plant life. Even the Earth crops they'd planted here tasted better. Paul had never much liked yellow squash, for example, but here it tasted amazing. It must be something in the soil, he figured.

What little fauna Demeter had was, well, little. The A-1, the biggest, baddest apex predator native to Demeter, was (drum roll, please) something called the Kangakitty. They were about the size of a rabbit and hopped like one. OK, they could actually jump about a meter into the air, gliding on membranes of skin that unfolded from their backs. And, yes, they were all needle-sharp teeth and claws. But they were also adorable. Sure, they were pests at times, occasionally getting hold of a chicken and dragging it off. But, think about it, the most dangerous animal on the planet – before humans showed up – was a three-pound ball of fluff that you could disarm by picking it up by the scruff of the neck.

This, more than anything about the planet, drove the ecologists (they had seven so far) completely bonkers. Sure, there was a food chain. Sure, there was a Great Web of Life. But everything on Demeter was either adorable, delicious, or both.

They called it Ryder's Paradox. It was named after Dr. Carl Ryder, whose grad student, Rachel St. Pierre, first noticed it. But, since cool things always seem to get named after old white men, it was called Ryder's Paradox.

Irene and Paul didn't give a crap about any of this, though. They were more concerned about making money hand over fist off the other colonists' obsession. Make no mistake, they loved Tatiana. They gave her the best care, the best education, the best of everything.

Glennis had been caring for Tatiana almost since she'd been born. Well, ever since Irene and Paul began making enough money to afford a full-time, live-in nanny, which wasn't long after. Glennis was wonderful with Tatiana, tutoring her, keeping her entertained, and, most importantly, keeping her grounded. It wasn't easy being the parents of the most famous person on the planet. Without Glennis guiding Tatiana (and Paul and Irene, for that matter), they could have easily ended up with an unmanageable monster. Instead, Tatiana was a well-behaved, talented, and thoughtful child.

Paul was still amazed at his daughter's talent. She could faithfully reproduce a scene she'd only viewed a few times or, in some cases, only once. Both he and Irene were – had been – urban planning specialists. Neither of them had anything you'd consider artistic talent. Fortunately, Glennis had been on hand to help the girl channel her creative energy into something concrete. Even so, Tatiana soon surpassed her teacher in artistic talent.

Irene and Glennis returned from whatever they'd been up to.

Irene smiled and winked at her husband. "How's our little Picasso?"

"More of a van Eyck, I'd say," Glennis interjected, nudging Irene playfully.

"Scribbling away, as per usual," Paul replied. He peered over Tatiana's shoulder. "Not entirely sure what she's drawing at the moment, though."

Tatiana looked up as if noticing the adults in the room for the first time. "They're called Zoomers."

"Why are they called Zoomers?" Glennis asked. The page was almost solid black. Distributed throughout the darkness, fading off into the distance, were hundreds of shiny, black pill-shaped objects. The one Tatiana had placed in the foreground had been drawn in cutaway view. Inside the pill's casing, what looked like a partially-formed figure slumbered, its limbs tucked into the vague semblance of a fetal position. "They look like they're all curled up and asleep."

"Of course they are, silly," Tatiana giggled. "It's too cold and dark to wake up yet."

"Like they're in stasis," Irene suggested.

Tatiana glanced at her mother, then looked to Glennis.

"We've talked about stasis, remember?" Glennis explained. "All the grownups who live on Demeter, everyone who came here on a ship, had to go into stasis. We slept for hundreds of years while the ships brought us here. We slept in pods much like those," she gestured to the drawing. "Is that what they are? Are they stasis pods?"

Tatiana's face scrunched up in concentration. "I suppose so. They sleep for a long time. They only wake up in the summer."

Paul shot a questioning look at Glennis, who replied with a shrug.

"Tatiana," Glennis said gently, "you know that Demeter doesn't have seasons like Earth did, right?"

It was true. Unlike Earth, Demeter had no axial tilt. It and its moon, Arion, were aligned precisely along the orbital plane. All the other planets in the system were perfectly aligned as well. It was all eerily precise. Every new moon brought a solar eclipse; every full moon, a lunar eclipse. And no axial tilt meant no seasons. Demeter was locked in eternal springtime.

"It has summer sometimes," Tatiana argued.

Paul was taken aback by his daughter's insistence. He crouched down beside her and hugged her shoulders. "Well, I've never seen a summer here," he said softly. "And I've been here six whole years. When does summer come, then?"

In response, Tatiana pulled out another drawing from the ones scattered about her. "Tomorrow."

Paul regarded this new picture. It showed a bright blue sky, with Demeter's sun, Helios, centered on the page. Blazing white light radiated from it. Positioned in front of Helios, dead-center, was Eos.

Eos was a tiny, dull red star, barely massive enough to manage fusion. Its paltry glow barely contributed to the light that warmed Demeter's surface. Unlike Demeter, Eos orbited Helios in a wild, wobbling pattern, crossing above or below its disc most times, sometimes grazing its edge, distorting the light slightly.

In the six years they'd been on Demeter, Paul had never heard nor seen Eos cross directly in front of Helios (not that he spent a lot of time staring at the suns). It must happen occasionally, he supposed.

"That's a lovely picture, dear," he said, giving Tatiana a

squeeze. "And that's going to happen tomorrow?"

She nodded. "Mmm hmm."

"Well, won't that be a sight!" he said, staring at the picture.

That evening, after Glennis had put Tatiana to bed, the three adults sifted through her drawings, assessing them for marketability.

"She seems to be drifting away from realism and experimenting in surrealism," Glennis commented. "Look at this one."

She held up a picture of the Verde Mountains at night, the sky heavy with storm clouds, bolts of red lightning silhouetting the mountains against the ruddy glow.

"Tatiana's never seen a thunderstorm," she said. "We've never had anything worse than a light sprinkle here. And, since when is lightning red? It's not like her to draw something she's never seen before."

"First the sleeping 'Zoomers,' then the whole 'summer' thing, now red lightning thunderstorms?" Paul gathered up more of Tatiana's drawings. "Let's see what else is in here."

The pictures she drew during the day were surreal, disturbing, and even violent in some cases. Several showed animal carcasses stripped down to the bone. Others showed trees, broken, torn to splinters.

Several showed Helios, high above the mountains, partially obscured by huge flocks of what looked like birds, their shapes too indistinct to identify. Demeter had no birds. Nothing here flew except a few pollinating insect-like bugs. Kangakitties didn't really count, of course. They could barely glide more than a dozen meters, even with a decent updraft.

Paul held up the drawing. "What do you think these are supposed to be?"

"She mentioned the Zoomers were waking up," Glennis noted. "Maybe that's what they look like when they're awake."

"Or maybe those are their ships," Paul said. "They're supposed to be in stasis, right?"

Irene shrugged. "Or maybe we're taking this a bit too seriously," she said. "These could be just some fantastical musings of a six-year-old. She does have a vivid imagination, after all."

"Yeah, about that..." Glennis began, scrolling through her teaching tablet. "Apparently, Helios and Eos will be in conjunction tomorrow. It's a big deal among the astronomy community."

"We have an astronomy community?" Irene interjected.

"Apparently," Glennis continued. "They're planning a viewing party for noon tomorrow. Distributing protective eyewear and everything."

"A party where everyone stares at the sun," Paul said, shaking his head. "So, Tatiana somehow knew about the conjunction, even though none of us did?"

"She could have found out about it through the news feeds," Glennis suggested. "I encourage her to read as much as possible."

Paul nodded, feeling a little relieved. "So, there's no reason to assume all of this other stuff is real, then." He gestured to the sheets containing the considerably more distressing images.

Glennis chuckled. "Not unless a freak thunderstorm with red lightning suddenly crops up overnight."

Her statement was punctuated by a distant rumble of thunder.

"Shit," she opined.

They watched through the rear patio doors as the storm gathered over the mountains to the east. Dark clouds lit up with flashes of red lightning. Rain began to spatter on the decking. Concentric rings radiated outward on the surface of the swimming pool where heavy raindrops landed.

"Think we should tell someone?" Paul asked.

Irene snorted. "Tell them what? Oh, hey, our daughter... you know, the famous Tatiana Portner? Yeah, well, not only is she the first person born on Demeter and a talented artist, but now it turns out she's a fortune teller too. I know, right? Who'd've guessed? Anyway, some creatures called Zoomers are coming out of stasis and are going to invade Demeter. Real gruesome stuff, I'm afraid. Alien invasion, cattle mutilations, the whole shebang."

Paul sighed. "When you put it that way, it sounds ridiculous, doesn't it? So, what do we do, just wait and see what happens?"

"I don't see how much more we could do," Glennis said, tapping at her tablet. "But I'm going to put a question out to the astronomy community, asking if the conjunction could be causing the storm and what, if anything, it might have to do with 'summer.' See if anyone responds."

It rained all night. Paul tried to get some sleep but wasn't very successful. Irene and Glennis seemed to be having similar problems.

Just before dawn, Glennis burst into their bedroom. "Tatiana's missing. I couldn't sleep, so I went to check on her. I've looked all over the house. I can't find her anywhere."

Irene threw on a robe. "OK, let's go over the house again, inside and out."

Fifteen frantic minutes later, Paul called out, "Found her!"

Tatiana was in the backyard, just beyond the fenced-in pool, hip-deep in a hole in the ground, still in her pajamas, and covered head-to-toe in mud.

Paul ran out into the yard, his bare feet squelching on the muddy, rain-soaked ground. At least it wasn't raining anymore. He slipped his hands under Tatiana's arms and lifted her out of the hole.

"What are you doing out here, kiddo?" he said.

She stared at him blankly for several seconds, then blinked. "Digging a hole."

"Why would you want to do that?" he asked.

She shrugged. "It's summer. You dig holes in summer."

"Hard to argue with that," he said. He picked her up again, cradling her in his arms, and carried her back into the house.

When they got inside, he set her on the floor and looked down. Both of them were covered in mud.

"I'm going to need a shower," he said. "Glennis, could you help Tatiana clean up, please? She's in dire need of a bath."

"I'll say," Glennis agreed and led Tatiana away.

"What was she doing out there?" Irene asked.

"Digging a hole."

"With her bare hands?"

"Apparently," Paul replied, stripping off what clothing he had on and stepping into the shower. "She was making good progress too. Half a meter deep and big enough for her to lie down in."

"Ugh, don't even joke about that," Irene said, gingerly picking up Paul's sodden clothes and dumping then in the hamper. "I mean, there's a time and place for graveyard humor, and this isn't it."

"Wasn't implying she was digging her own grave, dear," Paul called out from the shower. "Just giving a rough approximation of the hole's dimensions."

"Nevertheless," Irene retorted, "you could have used better phrasing."

She paused. "What now?"

Paul shut off the water and grabbed a towel. "What?"

Then he heard it: a distant low, droning hum. "What the hell is that?"

"If I had to guess, and given how things have been going lately," Irene said, "I'd say it's the Zoomers, come to invade the planet."

As the sun rose, Paul noticed the weather was unusually warm. "I guess this would be that 'summer' that Tatiana was talking about."

He glanced over at his daughter, who had her face pressed up against the patio door glass, looking at the mountains to the east.

The droning was getting louder. Whatever was coming would be here soon.

"Yeah, the astronomy buffs are arguing about what's causing the excess heat," Glennis said, flipping through her tablet. "They all agree that Eos is focusing Helios' light on the planet, but there's a difference of opinion on how it's doing that. Some say it's gravitational lensing; others say Eos isn't massive enough and that it must be an atmospheric effect."

Irene shook her head. "Rearranging the deck chairs on the Titanic. The world's about to end, and they're arguing about optical effects."

"Well, what are we doing about it?" Paul asked.

Irene stepped into the kitchen and pulled out a couple glasses. "Me, I'm breaking out the good wine. Anyone care to join me?"

Paul realized that Irene was probably right. They were facing an unknown threat, and the best they could do was ride it out. On the other hand, he felt she had to do something, even if it turned out to be ultimately unproductive. He wasn't sure which strategy was better if he were honest with himself. What if he exhausted himself running around now, only to be too tired to do something when it counted?

By noon, the sun had become blazingly bright, and the droning had become unbearably loud. Paul found it necessary to shout to be heard.

"Well, the world hasn't ended yet!" he pointed out.

"Give it time!" Irene shouted back, pouring another glass of Demeter's finest Merlot.

There was a sudden drop in temperature, accompanied by an abrupt dimming of the light outside. Something splashed into the pool.

Paul joined Tatiana at the patio doors to investigate. He pulled her away just before something large bashed against the glass, causing it to rattle alarmingly. The thing bounded away before Paul could get a good look at it.

Soon enough, though, there were plenty of opportunities to view the creatures. Hundreds, thousands of them swarmed across their property, half-hopping, half-flying, stopping only long enough to eat anything even vaguely edible. Grass, trees, small animals...

Paul recalled Tatiana's picture of a cow carcass. He tried not to imagine what these things would do to a human out in the open.

"Holy shit!" Glennis exclaimed, staring out the back door.

Paul turned to see the shattered remains of the pool shed falling to the ground as a Zoomer erupted from beneath it. That could just have easily been a bedroom or right beneath where he was standing. The Zoomers hadn't just been buried in the plains east of the mountains. They were in the ground everywhere.

"Everyone stay indoors," Irene said as if anyone had any inclination of stepping outside. "Glennis, could you get the word out for people to collect as many plants and animals as possible and store them in whatever shelter they can? I doubt a wooden barn would stand up to these things, but brick, steel, and glass seem to slow them down." She swept up Tatiana and headed for an interior room.

Paul and Glennis followed.

Paul had a brief flash of memory from his childhood. Tornado drills. Head for the basement if you have one; an interior room if you don't.

They had to turn on the lights in the house, even though it was noon. The Zoomers were blotting out the sun, as strong as it was.

Those things out there... they looked like nightmare versions of Kangakitties. They were much larger, for one thing. As big as a small child, so maybe twenty kilos, assuming a similar body density. Paul guessed the house could hold up to that. They didn't seem to be actively attacking the building, at least. What damage they'd sustained seemed to come from the creatures – the Zoomers – blundering into the house as they ravaged their way through Eleusis.

"Tatiana," he ventured, "Are those things outside the Zoomers you mentioned yesterday?"

She nodded. "They're awake now."

"Yes, they are," Paul agreed. "They were in stasis pods up until summer started, right?"

Another nod. "They sleep until summer."

"But I didn't see any space ships," Paul said. "Did they land their ships on the other side of the mountains?"

Tatiana shook her head. "No, daddy. They didn't come from ships."

"Oh, I see," Paul said. "Do you know where they came from, then?"

"Mmm hmm," she replied. "Don't you remember? I showed you the picture. They were in the dark, under the ground."

Paul felt his mouth go dry. "They've been here, on Demeter, the entire time? Ever since we arrived?"

Another nod. "They sleep most of the time. They only wake up for summer."

"Glennis," Paul said, his voice shaking, "I don't suppose those astronomy folks happen to know how often these conjunctions happen, do they?"

"Uh..." Glennis flipped through articles on her tablet.

"Looking..."

The lights flickered, went out, then gradually came back to life. One of the Zoomers must have bounced off a transformer.

"Shit," Glennis muttered. "Lost my connection."

"Glennis said a bad word," Tatiana pointed out.

Paul hugged her. "Yes, she did. She's very upset. We all are."

"Because of the Zoomers?"

"Yes. Because of the Zoomers."

"It's OK, daddy," Tatiana said. "They'll go back to sleep tomorrow when summer's over."

"OK, back online," Glennis announced. "Looks like about every fifteen years, give or take. Eos has to cross the orbital plane at just the right time of year in order to cause the lensing effect. Oh, and Emergency Management is already looking into recovery efforts. It's going to be a rough couple of months, but we should be OK. Beef's going to be in short supply for a while, I'm afraid. The next colony ship is due in a couple months. That'll help replenish the livestock."

"So, not the end of the world, then," Irene said. "Should've stuck to the cheap wine."

Paul glanced at her. "You're being awfully cavalier about all this."

She waved it off. "We'll be fine. We've got a steady, reliable income and a ton of cash socked away. Sure, we'll need to rent some maintenance robots to repair the house, but that'll barely make a dent. And we've got fifteen years to prepare for the next round."

"Or," Paul ventured, "we've got fifteen years to dig up and destroy all the pods."

"The ecologists might have something to say about that," Glennis noted. "After all, we have no idea what sort of effect that would have on Demeter's other species. For all we know, secretions from those pods they sleep in provide nutrients or microorganisms essential to the survival of the plant life here."

Paul sighed. "So we could be stuck with them, then. Great. I should've known this planet was too good to be true."

The droning had tapered off as the Zoomers ran out of food and moved on, either down the shoreline or back towards the mountains. Paul went to the front door and took a peek outside. If it weren't for the rich, dark soil, he'd have thought he was looking out into a desert. He wondered how long it'd take for the peach apple grove to regrow. Months? Years? Things did seem to grow pretty fast here. Maybe Irene was right. Maybe they'd be OK.

He noticed a few Kangakitties bouncing around. How had they avoided being eaten? Maybe the Zoomers didn't like the taste of them? Maybe Kangakitties had a way of fighting back?

He noticed a few of them – about half of the ones he could see were digging in the barren soil. They dug down until they were neck-deep, then pulled the dirt on top of them, burying themselves alive.

"Hey!" he shouted. "Come have a look at this." Irene and Glennis came up behind him.

"Huh," Glennis said. "You don't suppose they're going to turn into Zoomers, do you?"

Irene shrugged. "We could wait a few days, dig one up, and see if the little bugger's spun a pod around itself, I suppose."

"Sounds like a plan," Paul said.

Glennis stared out the front door, watching the Kangakitties.

"So, now what?"

"First thing, I'm going to call for some maintenance robots to patch up the house," Irene said. "Best to get on the waiting list as soon as possible. Maybe slip a bit of cash into the right hands to get bumped up in the queue."

Paul nodded. "Oh! And make sure they fill in that hole in the backyard. Don't want anyone falling in."

By late afternoon, there were maintenance robots climbing all over the house, patching up dents, and replacing broken glass. Irene must have slipped quite a lot of cash into the right hands.

By the time they'd finished dinner, things seemed pretty much back to normal, as long as you ignored the fact that the world outside the house was almost completely devoid of life.

Exhausted, everyone went to bed early and slept in the following morning.

"Has anyone seen Tatiana?" Glennis asked. "She's not in her bed."

"Oh no, not again," Paul grumbled, heading for the backyard.

But, no, Tatiana wasn't digging a hole in the yard. Then where was she?

After they'd combed through the house and surrounding property, Glennis called the police and reported her missing.

"It's not just Tatiana," she said. "The police have already received dozens of reports of missing children this morning. And, get this, all of them are six or younger."

Paul stared at her.

Six or younger. All born on Demeter. What was it about this planet? First, ravenous monsters that swarm every fifteen years before buggering off to their graves again. And now, what, something comes in the middle of the night and kidnaps all the kids born here?

Graves.

Big enough for her to lie down in.

No.

No, no, no.

Paul rushed out the back door and fell to his knees, clawing at the dirt.

He caught Glennis out of the corner of his eye.

"Well, don't just stand there," he snapped. "Get some help."

"Oh shit," Glennis breathed. She turned and ran back inside.

A few minutes later, a maintenance robot showed up and started digging under Paul's directions.

"Be careful," he told it. "She could still be alive down there."

He watched on, along with Irene and Glennis, as the robot scraped away dirt, layer by layer.

The robot's claws clacked against something hard and smooth.

"OK, stop," Paul commanded, and the robot backed away.

Paul scraped the remaining dirt away with his hands and wrestled the pod out of the hole.

"So it's just some Kangakitty that happened to dig in the same spot," Irene said.

"It looks too big to be a Kangakitty," Glennis pointed out.

"It can't be Tatiana," Irene protested. "It's a pod. Six-year-old children can't just spin a cocoon around themselves. How would she even know how to do that?"

For all we know, secretions from those pods they sleep in provide nutrients or microorganisms... Paul heard voices at the front door.

"I also called for medical assistance," Glennis explained. "Just in case."

She went to greet the med techs and bring them into the back yard.

One of the med techs crouched down and ran a scanner wand over the pod's surface, watching intently as a 3D view assembled itself on its viewscreen.

She looked up. "I don't know. All that's showing up is a mass of cells, no differentiation. Could be anything in there."

"See?" Irene said, desperation creeping into her voice. "It could be anything."

Paul nodded. It could be anything. And Irene was right. Human children didn't go around spinning themselves into cocoons. Earth children didn't, anyway.

But Tatiana and the other missing children had spent their entire lives on Demeter. Breathing its air, drinking its water, eating its food. Demeter was in every cell of their bodies.

Provide nutrients…

…or microorganisms…

It must be something in the soil…

No, children couldn't spin cocoons around themselves. But children didn't suddenly know about conjunctions and thunderstorms and plagues of Zoomers, either.

Zoomers looked like nightmare versions of Kangakitties, and he'd just yesterday witnessed Kangakitties burying themselves. So, what, did Kangakitties bury themselves in the ground and, fifteen years later, Zoomers come out?

Paul recalled how caterpillars, inside their cocoons, turned into goo before re-forming themselves into butterflies. But Zoomers were nothing like butterflies. More like locusts. Big, grotesque locusts, all teeth and claws.

He looked down at the pod, its smooth, shiny, black surface yielding no clues to what, or who was inside.

Yes, anything could be in there, but it was probably Tatiana.

He was finding it all so difficult to process. He'd lost his little girl. Right now, he didn't give two shits about the fame or the money. He just wanted his little girl back.

He'd lost Tatiana, but here she was, right in front of him. She wasn't gone, not really. It was so easy, so seductive, to think of Tatiana tucked away in there, in stasis, his little sleeping princess.

A mass of cells, no differentiation…

He shook his head to clear his thoughts. No. Whatever was in this pod wasn't Tatiana. No more than what was in a cocoon was a caterpillar. And what it would become was anyone's guess. Probably not a butterfly, though.

He tried to imagine what would come out of these pods – the ones containing the colonists' children – when they hatched fifteen years from now. Would they recognize their parents? Even if they did, would they show them any deference, any mercy?

Paul sat there in the mud, staring at the ground, gently caressing the pod's carapace, waves of grief and dread alternately washing over him. He decided, on the whole, that he wasn't really looking forward to next summer.

GRAVE'S EDGE
BY ALEX O'NEAL

Papua New Guinea.

I knew I was a vampire because I crawled out of my grave.

They piled the dirt over me despite my cries, and eventually, I realized I was dead. I had heard stories of souls who died and did not know it. For a brief second, I felt myself lucky for having the insight, and then a clod of dirt hit my eye. I covered my face with my arms and my burr-ridden wrap.

They did it at night, which is perhaps why they didn't bury me too deeply. My daughter cried and shooed the children back to the house as her husband shoveled. Shortly after I was covered, she broke down completely, and her husband dropped the shovel and comforted her. I heard their footsteps recede, imagining his arm around her as he told her he would finish in the morning. I noticed I was still sucking at the bit of air slipping under the dirt-covered wool. Old habits die hard. I waited a while, hoping I would move on to oblivion. I felt the ground shake as a car passed on a nearby road. I wondered if this was what it was like to live in a cemetery.

I was not in a cemetery. I was in a shallow grave in the woods across the street from my daughter's home. I expected she would visit at times and cry, and I would listen and answer and go unheard. I had been unheard for some time, on my pallet in their hut, steadily growing smaller and bonier and weaker.

I had the slims, you see, the wasting disease that brought the foreign doctors with their needles and the foreign reporters with their cameras, and which they said passed through the blood or the remnants of love. Perhaps they were right. They came to the southern highlands and were kind, and sometimes even tried to learn our language in addition to the pidgin we all shared, the better to help us. But they were wrong. I think I got it from hating my husband. He was beautiful and blessed with a voice like a growling purr, soothing and predatory, and too many women fell victim to its persuasions. I hated him for it, even after he died wasting as I would, and what god could forgive a mother who hated the man that gave her the loving child of her heart? Obviously, not mine.

So I worked until I had to sit down, and sat until I had to lie down and lay until I died. And now I was in the underworld, beneath footsteps and any other living sound, listening to cars.

My poor daughter. How distraught she must have been to find my body. On the floor, a little stiller than usual. I wondered how long I lay before someone noticed. Probably not too long. Someone was always checking on me: I would feel a palm against my forehead, or my blanket tucked a little more securely, or water at my lips, and I would open my eyes to see my daughter, or her daughter, looking back at me with strained relief.

My body. Oh, what foolishness—I did not have to stay here straining to hear earthworms. I did not have to remain in my grave. Every ghost story I knew freed the soul from its body. I could rise up, and leave this traitorous shell behind.

So I did. It was very difficult; I was very weak. I lifted my funeral shroud up carefully from my face, trying to make the dirt fall away from me. A little hit my mouth, and I began to cough, which seemed terribly unfair. I realized I had to get used to being dead and laughed while I coughed at how the ghost stories didn't talk about this. Of course they didn't. The storytellers were alive.

I sat up with difficulty, then used the crumbling edge of the grave to raise myself up. I had not walked in weeks—months, maybe—and this hurt. If I had been alive, I would have said it was impossible. But dead, I knew such considerations were the lying of my mind and would pass. I stood, teetering, for a moment. In front of me were branches, and through them, I could see the light seeping past the door of my old home. As I watched, it went out, and I was left with only moonlight. I debated looking at my body behind me. I was afraid. Even though death had come and gone, and I was still moving and aware, something about seeing death written on my features terrified me, and made my gut ache and my breath catch like it hadn't in decades.

But I had to look. Really, who couldn't? And turning to look behind me, I became a pillar of salt.

My body was missing. Or rather, it wasn't missing. It was standing.

I stood for some time, absorbing this. I don't know how long. It seemed there was a very long pause in my mind, and all that occupied it was the empty grave I was trying not to see. Something hovered in my head, demanding my attention, and I tried to avoid it by studying the grave, the bits of brown and roots and gray leaves where the dim light struck, the abyss of the shadows where it did not. But I could not evade it forever.

I was the undead. I was the monster. My hatred had been even stronger than I had realized and had cursed me beyond the grave. The very fact I had crawled from my grave bore witness that I was the blood-sucking terror of the night. Doomed, eventually, by hunger and my curse to hunt the people I had lived with all my life.

What to do? I had to leave before I lost the habits of life and began to practice the ways of death. My daughter and her husband would be in danger then. My granddaughter! They had no idea such a terrible person had lain on their floor all that time, or the man my daughter married would have removed my head and removed the danger.

I began to totter toward the road, aching with each step. I bit my lip and told myself not to curse. I blinked a little at the few tears that managed to squeeze into my eyes. I was already thirsty. It was not for blood, not yet, but it would be.

A car came down the road and slowed as it saw me beneath the edge of the trees. It was two of the foreign helpers, a man, and a woman. The one on my side of the road rolled down the window.

"Do you need help, mother?" The friendly intimacy of his tone struck me like a slap.

I gathered my voice carefully. "I need to leave." Like my legs, my voice was feeble. I would need sustenance soon.

"Are you lost?"

"No, I just need to leave." I hoped they would take me far enough away that I would not endanger my village. I hoped I would control myself and not harm my benefactors, but if not, better foreign strangers than family and friends. I took a step toward the car and stumbled. The car door belonging to the friendly voice opened, and the young man came out and took my arm.

"Are you all right? You're covered in dirt—did you fall? Are you hurt?"

"No." I was anxious to get into the car before he looked past me.

He looked past me, of course, and saw the man-sized blackness in the ground. "What the hell?" He raised his voice somewhat to be heard in the car. "Hey, Paula, get over here!"

"Please, no. Just take me away."

He craned his head down to look into my face. His expression was remarkably like the anxious care of my daughter. "Is that a grave?"

I didn't speak. A middle-aged woman came up with a flashlight. "Do you need help, Reghu?" She shone the flashlight on me, revealing the dirt covering my shroud. "You poor thing, you're filthy. Where is your home? Can we take you there?"

The young man spoke quietly. "Paula, take a look behind us."

The flashlight danced beyond us, uncovering the grave. The woman's other hand went to the camera around her neck, flipping it on and snapping off the lens cap as if part of herself, even as she gasped.

I sighed in defeat. Now they would know what I was and would never take me anywhere. I was doomed to kill where I loved.

She handed over the flashlight to the man. "Hold this on the grave. I want to shoot it with the flashlight and then a couple with the flash." She glanced at me. "And something with both her and the grave."

"Paula, she's right here. You can't talk about people like they're elements in a still life."

"I'm not still. I'm not alive," I mumbled to myself.

"What was that?" he asked, face even more filled with concern. I kept silent. Maybe they would take me anyway. They didn't seem to realize the monster I had become. The woman stepped back and took a photo of the young man and myself, with the grave just behind. She leaned in to take a close-up of the earth-stained fabric and my hand, and I shook the dirt off at her irritably.

"Please take me away."

She let go of the camera, letting it hang, focusing on me. "Ma'am, were you in that grave?" She paused, and swallowed. "Did someone bury you?"

"Please, I need to leave. I don't want to hurt anyone."

Her eyebrows went up. "I'm sorry, but you don't really look like a threat."

The man cut her off. "Let's get her in the car so she can sit down, Paula. Then we can go someplace safe and talk more. I don't really like standing in the dark near a newly dug grave, do you?"

The woman nodded. "You're right. You know, I'd heard about families doing things like this to AIDS victims, but I thought it was just a rumor."

"They buried me wrong," I explained as the two led me to the car.

"Yes, it was wrong of them to bury you," the young man—hardly more than a boy—said, correcting me gently.

"No, they buried me wrong," I repeated. "It wasn't their fault."

"It wasn't their fault they buried you alive?" the woman exclaimed. The boy shot her a warning look.

"I'm not alive, but they didn't know what they were burying. Please," I said as I sank down gratefully onto the car seat and felt my legs lifted and placed in the car. "Please just take me away. I don't want to hurt anyone." I looked earnestly into the young man's eyes. "Would you cut off my head, please?"

"What?" They were shocked.

"I'm dead, and I can't leave, and if someone doesn't cut off my head, I'll hurt someone."

The woman shook her head, and the young man put his hand on my shoulder. "You're not dead, mother."

"Of course I'm dead. My daughter wouldn't bury me alive!"

"They made a terrible mistake. But you're alive."

"It wasn't a mistake, Reghu, we've heard about this before."

"God, Paula, be quiet, please. You're not helping." He paused. "And now we've woken up the people across the street."

I looked at my home. He was right. A light was moving in my

old home. "Please," I said, "let's go. They can't know I'm like this!"

"They'll know you're alive as soon as they see the grave, mother."

"But I'm not alive! I am undead," I said, watching with dread as the door flap opened, "and I am hungry and thirsty. If we don't leave, I will hurt my family."

My son-in-law emerged, carrying his machete fearfully. He had probably watched the car a few minutes before emerging to see what was happening. He might not have seen me since I was on the other side of the car. "Please, quick! Quick!" I begged.

The woman walked around to talk to the man who had buried me. He tucked his machete at his waist, unafraid of a woman. Initially quiet, voices were quickly raised, and my son-in-law began to yell, trying to walk around to my side of the car. I stopped listening. The boy and the woman tried to stand in his way, but too soon, he stood before me, his tattooed face twisted by pain and fear.

"I'm sorry," I said before he could speak. "I didn't want you to know. You should've taken precautions."

He stared. Then, to the young man, "She walked here? She stood on her own?"

"Yes."

I watched comprehension bring horror. "You knew it might happen," I said. "When my husband got the slims, we all thought it came from the witch in the next village. She had a reason to hate

57

him. Who's to say the curse didn't fall on me as well?" I was sympathetic but angry, too. "Why didn't you stop this?"

"What was I supposed to do?" he burst out. "Cut off your head? You should have died!"

"Yes, cut off my head!" I was very angry. "I was dead. I was not going to miss it, was I? Now I'm undead, and I'm thirsty." I leaned toward him. "Thirsty!" The fear in his eyes pleased me; he had not been patient with me the past weeks, I did not contribute, and I ate their food, and I smelled. "Thirsty…" I said again and leaned back against the car seat, looking at the woman and the boy.

"Take me away from here. Please."

"No, you can't!" my son-in-law said. "She will kill you!"

"She couldn't hurt a fly," the woman said. "She could barely walk to the car."

"She hasn't walked in months! She had the slims, the wasting disease. We buried her. She died! She should have stayed dead! Alive, she could not have walked here!"

"Sir, your mother—"

"She's not my mother! She is my wife's mother, and she's cursed." The noise had brought out my daughter, and he yelled at her to go back inside. Suddenly he fumbled for the knife at his waist. "I should have done this before. I didn't think it would happen."

Both the woman and the boy grabbed at him, but he brandished the machete at them, and they backed off, protesting.

"Sir, you can't do this! She's not some kind of vampire. She's alive! You made a mistake burying her, and she came back."

"There's no mistake," I said. "He's right. He should end me now while he still can."

"Mother?" My daughter had come around the back of the car. She was holding a gun more nervously than my son-in-law carried his machete. It was an old one, hidden in the home for decades, found by my father during the years the Japanese invaded. "Mother?"

And then my daughter was on her knees beside the car, head in my lap, crying and begging forgiveness. I stroked her hair, soothing her. I told her there was nothing to forgive. She had not cursed me. Her father had done that. She looked up at me. "I love you, dear," I said. "But you must let your husband do this thing."

"What thing?"

My son-in-law came forward and took her hand.   "Come away from her. She is undead."

"No, she's alive! You know she's alive!"

"No, she's not! She walked to the car. She walked, do you hear?"

I interrupted them. "Of course I'm not alive. Would my daughter have buried me alive?"

My daughter looked at me, stricken. Understanding seemed to seep into her features, but not the fear I dreaded. The two foreigners were silent now, watching. I looked at my son-in-law. "Will you cut off my head?"

He nodded and gingerly offered a hand to help me from the car.

I stood a little more easily this time. The boy seemed about to speak, but the woman laid her hand on his arm. Shaking, my daughter pointed the gun she barely knew how to hold at them. I walked back toward the grave with my son-in-law.

We stopped at the edge. He looked at me with compassion.

"You are ready?"

"Yes. Should I kneel or lie down?"

"If you can kneel, it would help."

"You will have to help me do it, then. I have not fed, and I'm weak." He touched me again to help me kneel, then stood back, still afraid of me. I looked at my daughter, who glanced back at me and then looked away quickly. "Stand between us, please." My son-in-law complied. I bowed my head. The two foreigners watched uncomprehendingly, or rather as if they could not bear what they understood.

I looked down at the grave's emptiness. I was glad I would be leaving myself behind. Glad I was near my home, glad my family was safe. If my son had not come out, how long would it have been before the monster that crawled out of my grave took over and hurt them?

I looked up at my son. "Take care of my daughter."

"I will."

"Thank you." I bowed my head.

TRICK AND TREAT
BY JEANNE FRANC

Halloween dawned bright as early light snaked through the slats of Cedric's bedroom blinds. But the note lying on the pillow beside him soured the delight he felt on this most wonderful of days. Somehow, an unseen, unheard intruder had again sneaked through his house while he slept and left this inscrutable message on his bed.

"LOVE .. ... MONSTERS".

Cedric screamed with rage. 'Enough!'

Identical note: same words, same dots. He had a niggling feeling the dots were important, but a magnifying glass failed to reveal anything special about them. He crumpled the flimsy paper and then angrily ripped it into tiny shreds. Three nights in a row! And he never heard a sound! How were they getting in?

Cedric forced a calming breath. 'Enough,' he repeated. Tonight he would catch the intruder.

***

Street noises died away as the last of the trick-or-treaters drifted home. Cedric locked the front door and strode into the kitchen. He grabbed his largest knife and headed for the den, determined to stay awake all night. He stretched out on the lumpy couch, ignoring the spring that dug into his back. He closed his eyes and focused on the kitchen clock's faint, monotonous rhythm. Soon his thoughts drifted away, as they always did on this special night, back twenty years. It's true, he thought, you never forget your first.

Sweet Rosalie.

At seventeen, she was tall, awkward, shy, and unsure enough of her femininity. Naïve and trusting, she believed him when he swore he loved her, and would marry her right after high school. Cedric smiled, recalling how he would laugh after he left her at her front door, dreamy-eyed and whispering his name.

His pulse raced at the memory of the phone call he made on that long-ago Halloween night to tell Rosalie it was over. He was taking Juanita to the school dance. He could still hear her sobs pleading for him to come back. When he laughed, she called him a 'monster.'

When news swept through town the next morning that she had tied a cement block around her waist before she waded into the lake, an unholy rapture thrilled Cedric. His life suddenly had meaning.

The coroner's verdict was suicide while of unsound mind.

Unsound mind!

Cedric guffawed. He had found dozens of Rosalie's over the years (thank you, internet!). He mentally congratulated himself on his brilliant acumen for teasing out those malleable personalities and grooming them to his will before fracturing their glass egos.

Over the years, he had perfected his technique. A week or two before Halloween, he stopped responding to calls and texts. When he did reply, it was terse, formal: 'caught in traffic, held up at work, called to a family emergency.' A couple of days before the big night, he would return to his warm, flowery language, apologize, invite her to a costume party, and hint he had something special for her. A quick gasp told him she was imagining a ring.

When the big night arrived, he sat home and imagined her pacing the floor as the minutes sped by, dressed in some ludicrous costume while she waited for him, her unanswered texts more urgent. Then he sent his final message.

'It's over. Found somebody new.'

His latest was Natalie. Soft brown hair, big doe eyes. Diamond chip embedded in the tip of her tongue. He licked his lips at the memory of the pleasure that diamond had given him.

Craziest one of the lot, he mused. When he stopped answering her calls, he expected Natalie to be curious at first, then bewildered, then hurt. But she went straight to desperate. She threatened him and herself, screamed he was a liar when he offered his excuses

Should have seen she was ready to crack into a thousand pieces. Candles always burning, incense clouding the bedroom, strange little altars clustered together on mantels and shelves. He had even overheard her chanting nonsensical gibberish one night before she realized he was in the room.

Cedric had just sent his placating text three nights ago about the party when a friend called. Natalie had already dived from her fifteenth-floor balcony.

He pouted. Now his perfect suicide Hallowe'en record was spoiled. Also, she had robbed him of the humor of knowing his weeping victim paced the floor dressed for a fake party.

A new thought struck Cedric. He didn't have Natalie to goad over the edge, true, but maybe her death heralded a new 'hands-on' twist in his life. The first would be the sneak he was waiting for.

Cedric chuckled. 'I'll be a new monster.'

Something soft landed on his face, and Cedric screeched and flailed at his eyes. When his fingers closed on a flimsy piece of paper, he shot up and turned on the table lamp.

"LOVE .. ... MONSTERS".

Cedric knuckled his eyes. The 'O' in 'MONSTERS' was shifting, widening. Cedric gaped as it opened further, revealing a vast, moist blackness. A red dot appeared in the middle. Cedric gulped as a row of tiny white stubs appeared along the top, then the bottom. They grew and sharpened.

The first two dots begin to shimmer, then burst into letters:

"T."

"O."

The red spot wriggled and wormed toward his face, elongating into a thick, coiled band. It uncurled, and Cedric recoiled in horror. It looked unnervingly like a tongue.

The last three dots shimmered, and formed:

"E."

"*A.*"

"*T.*"

Frozen with fear, he stared at the needle-sharp teeth coming closer and closer.

The last thing Cedric saw before the black maw engulfed his head was a sparkling diamond chip embedded in the moist tip.

FALL FROM GRACE
BY JIM KIERNAN

Military service was always something that interested me. Sure, kids dream about being AstroFor Pilots, or CDF Patrollers, but I was curious about the Civil Defense Force's Operator Corps: the men and women who see ground combat. They're the ones who take out valuable targets so the Terrestrial Shock Troops can be virtually unstoppable on the ground. My mother knew how much I wanted this. She was hesitant at first, but I wore her down over time. Eventually, I convinced her to accompany me to a recruiting station so I could enlist early, at 17.

The enlistment process was about what I expected. I spent most of it undergoing physical and intellectual tests. In the second half, I was interviewed; they wanted to know where my loyalties lay, and if I was truly a good fit for the Civil Defense Forces.

They decided I was.

Several weeks later, during Basic Training Preparation (something reserved for early enlistees), I was approached by an officer wearing patches on his uniform I didn't recognize.

"Are you Morgan Farris?" he asked.

"I am," I told him.

"My name is Major Saren Mordock," he said, holding out his hand, which I shook. "May I speak with you in private?"

"Okay," I said, and he led me away from the main group and

around the side of a building, so we were out of sight.

"Are you aware there is treason within the Terrestrial Shock Troop Corps?" He asked.

"Uhh . . ." I stuttered. It was a large question to ask someone barely out of school, let alone someone hadn't graduated basic training. "I'm . . . aware that they are all conscripts. I could maybe see how some might be bitter about that."

Mordock grunted. "Indeed. Well, some are much more than bitter. Do you see that as a problem?"

"Absolutely." I nodded. "Most of them were going to rot away in prison or out on the streets. If you ask me, the Archonship gave them a purpose in life. They should be thankful."

"Couldn't have said it better myself," Mordock said with a smirk. "Your enlistment evaluation says you're more loyal and more intelligent than the average Civil Defense recruit."

"Really?"

"Really," Mordock repeated. "Perhaps you'd like a job with the CDF, that is . . . a bit more proactive in deterring treason within the Terrestrial Shock Troop Corps?"

"I'm listening," I said.

"I can't tell you more. You have to accept or decline right now." Mordock explained. "Just understand, if you accept, then you will be going into deep cover within the TSTC. You will have to fake your death. All of your family and friends with thinking you are dead, and it may be several standard decades, at the very least, before you're pulled out."

I opened my mouth to speak, but Mordock continued.

"But," he said, "you will be serving the Archon in a way that very few Gliesie citizens will ever have the honor, or even opportunity, to do. We are elite. Above the Operators. We are the Shadow Operatives."

I told him: "I accept."

***

I go to put my breakfast MRE pill in my mouth, but yawn. It's only my second time being reanimated from cryostasis, at least from a stasis period longer than a few days. It's not fun. I feel awful when I first wake up and then groggy for several hours after. We're on hour two.

Once I'm done yawning, I pop the pill into my mouth and swallow. That's more effort than it should be. My mouth is dry from the reanimation, and they don't give us fluids to take our MREs with. My teammate Kaed says they do this to keep us mad and ready to kill angels.

I look around the cafeteria and see Aster sitting off by herself, so I walk over and take a seat with her. "Hey, cribbie," I say, using the term the older troopers call us. It's not that they're calling us babies, but rather that we were conscripted young and are therefore more naïve.

"Hey, Kal," Aster says. She and I are the only new blood on our team, so we've somewhat bonded over that. "Have a good shower?"

"If you consider freezing cold water good, then yes," I answer, getting a smirk and a singular chuckle out of Aster.

"Aye, cribbies!" I hear, and I don't need to turn around to know it's Kaed, our team's marksman, but I turn around anyway. "You know Seera likes us to sit together at the beginning of the day."

"Sorry, Kaed," Aster says. "I couldn't see—"

"Follow me." Kaed waves his arms instructing us to follow.

Aster and I do as we're told. If being in the Fleet has taught me anything, it's that shock troopers have no qualms with using violence to get their way. It's like being in prison, if you were allowed to get pokked up and have sex with escorts . . . not that I know what prison is like, but some of the older troops have told me.

We get to the table, and the other half of our team is already seated. Foreman Seera, our team leader, is sitting straight with her fingers intertwined, looking at us with a cold patience. Yeoman Jerik, Seera's second-in-command, doesn't even seem to notice us. Then there's Yaro, who's a rifleman like me. Aster is our heavy weapon specialist.

"Hey, K-junior!" Yaro says to me. He calls me 'K-junior' because we already have someone with a 'K' name on the team. Yaro throws his MRE pill at me, which I catch despite my surprise. "Toss it at me. I'm gonna catch it with my mouth."

"Don't throw that, Trooper," Seera says, pointing at me. "Hand it back to him. Yaro, you'll take that pill like a pokkin' normal person, or I'll shove it down your throat."

"Hayu, Foreman!" Yaro and I answer.

I lean over and hand Yaro's pill back to him. He grabs my hand and pulls me in. "We can try it later at dinner." He winks.

Jerik slaps Yaro upside his head. "Ignore him, Kal."

"Hayu, Yeoman," I say.

"You two waiting for an invitation?" Seera asks, and I notice that Aster and I are still standing, so we take our seats at the table.

"I bumped into Supervisor Koreth on my way to the showers," Seera continues, referring to our unit commander. "He saved the exciting details for the briefing, but we're gonna see some serious combat this deployment."

"Nice!" Kaed says, sharing a giant grin with Yaro.

Seera narrows her vision at Aster and me. "You two prepped for that?"

"Hayu, Foreman!" Aster says.

"Mercy is weakness, Foreman!" I say, reciting the motto of the Terrestrial Shock Troop Corps.

"Easy to talk," Seera says. "But our last deployment was child's play. Type 0, Bronze Age. You understand they're not going to bow to us like gods this time, right?"

"Yes, Foreman," Aster and I answer in unison.

***

Half an hour later, we're all in the unit's auditorium, where

Supervisor Koreth will brief us on the deployment details, such as current military intel and each team's individual assignments. Of the three possible assignments a team can be given, I'm hoping for assault because those see the most action. Last time we were given strongpoint, which is basically just sitting outside of a metropolitan area and eliminating anyone trying to enter or leave. I was bored to tears.

"Good morning, troopers," Supervisor Koreth says, stepping up onto the podium with Foreman Seera. She's the most senior foreman in our unit, so she acts as the unit's second-in-command.

"Good morning, Supervisor!" The auditorium booms.

"Did you all sleep well?" Koreth asks, receiving some light laughter.

"Let's get to it." He holds up a remote and presses a button. A planet forms above the holoprojector on the stage with them. The holo never portrays the planet's size well, but it has blue oceans and green/brown continents. "This is our target. Civilization ranks a Type 1, Space Age infancy. AstroFor has already disabled their satellites and is in the process of eliminating any obvious air, naval, and nuclear assets. Our mission is the same as always: secure metropolitan areas, defeat any counterattacks and await further instructions from Civil Defense. Any questions?"

The room is silent. It was basically the same briefing as the last deployment. The only real difference being the civilization ranking and the fact that there will probably be actual metropolitan areas here.

"Alright, team assignments are as follows . . ." Koreth goes down the list of teams numerically. We're team 3, so we don't have to wait very long. "3/74," Koreth says, and I perk up. "Assault."

"Thank pok," Yaro subtly pumps his fist. I look over at him, and he and Kaed give each other a high five.

I look over at Aster, and she gives me a wink. "I hope you like blood on your boots."

I grin. "Same wager as last time?"

"Deal." She holds out her hand. I take it, but she holds it firm.

"Mech kills count as three."

"No fair," I object. "You'll already be stackin' bodies with that fusion compressor. Plus, we don't know how many of these angels it takes to operate one of their mechs."

"You gonna take one out with your stinger rifle?" she asks with a raised brow.

"Maybe," I shrug. "I've seen stinger rifles pierce mech armor before."

"Bullshit, where?" Aster squints.

"Indoc!" I say, referring to the training program child conscripts go through.

"I didn't see anything like that in Indoc," Aster says.

"Is there something you'd like to share with the rest of us, troopers?" Supervisor Koreth says, and I look up at the podium. He's staring directly at Aster and me, and Foreman Seera doesn't look very happy with us.

"Nothing, Supervisor," I say. "Sorry."

"No." Koreth shakes his head. "That looked like quite a debate. Let's hear it."

I look at Aster, and she gives me a look that tells me I'm speaking for the both of us now. "Well, Supervisor," I say, clearing my throat. "Me 'n Aster have a wager: whoever gets the most confirmed kills during the day drinks for free that night. We were sorting out the details."

Koreth smirks. "I like that. But why don't you shut the pok up while you're in my briefing room."

"Hayu, Supervisor!" Aster and I bark back.

***

"I'm tellin' you, mechs should count as two," Aster says, leaning against my attila link, which I'm sitting in.

"You said they should count as three before." I point out.

"I accept those terms," Aster says.

"Pok off." I laugh. "Mechs count as one."

"C'mon!" She objects, throwing her arms in the air. "You can't take out a mech with your stinger. Mechs should count as more."

"Give it a pokkin' rest," Kaed says, stopping at my link to stare at us. "If I hear any more about this, I'm gonna beat the shit outta both of you."

"Hey," Aster says, but Kaed is already climbing into his own attila link. She turns to me and leans in. "You ever get any funny feelings around Kaed?"

"No . . . what do you mean?"

"I don't know . . . I just get the feeling he might be . . ."

"Might be . . . what?"

"You know . . ."

"No . . ."

Aster leans in even closer and whispers. "A Ghost . . ."

"What?" I laugh. "Come on, Aster. He's not a Ghost."

"I mean, think about it. He's always so serious, he's a deadeye with that stinger, and—"

"You know what other profession that describes? A shock troop marksman." I smile with amusement.

"Pok off, Kal." She waves her hand at me dismissively.

"Seera's a lot like that too. You think she's a Ghost?"

Aster grunts. "Don't get me started," she says just as Seera comes around the corner behind her. "Type 0s are child's play, troopers!"

I swipe my hand across my throat, trying to tell her to shut up, but she doesn't get it. Seera winds up and smacks Aster across the side of her head.

"Worlds beyond!" Aster curses, grabbing her ear and looking at Seera with a look of betrayal. "Foreman, that pokkin' hurt!"

"Good," Seera says matter-of-factly. "Maybe next time you'll think before being a wiseass."

"Hayu, Foreman," Aster says, touching her rapidly reddening ear.

"Let's link up!" Seera booms.

"Hayu, Foreman!" I answer, looking back at Aster. "Don't worry about that ear. You won't feel it after you link up."

"Easy for you to say," she says, gritting her teeth. "See ya down there."

I lay back in my attila link, and the lid begins to fold over me. I close my eyes and let my mind go blank. It takes a few seconds, but I suddenly feel as though I'm falling down a pitch black, bottomless pit. It's odd to experience, but it's the correct sensation to have while the consciousness transfers from a physical body to an attila. Soon, I find myself in a tree line overlooking a large field. At the far edge of the field, perhaps a kilometer out is a town of some kind: our objective.

I look over and see the attilas of my teammates. Well, seeing isn't really the appropriate word for it. Each of our attilas are shielded by three energy shields and then concealed by something called a chameleon field, or cam field for short. These cam fields render us nearly invisible, save for a distinctive bending of light that is difficult to see or identify if you're not actively looking for it. In order for us to see our teammates, our attilas' Heads Up Displays, or HUDs, create light blue auras around other attilas. In the case of Foreman Seera, or other foremen for that matter, this aura is green to indicate leadership status.

Seera's attila is holding its hand up to its visual port, or v-port, wiggling its fingers. She then picks up her stinger rifle and charges it.

"Good idea," I think, accidentally sending it out over our

thought comms, which is how we're able to communicate with each other.

"What is?" Yeoman Jerik asks.

"Foreman's checking her weapon," I say, picking up my own stinger rifle and pulling the charging handle.

We then go through the process of checking our equipment. This is just a tedious step in our preparedness before starting our mission. We each take our turn examining our equipment and reporting back over thought comms whether or not the equipment is in working condition or if we've discovered or suspected a malfunction.

It all goes well. No issues reported.

"Okay," Seera says, turning and looking out at the town in the distance. There are columns of black smoke rising up from the buildings, and even from this distance, it's easy to see that none of them are in one piece anymore. "AstroFor did a number on that met."

"Yeah, they did," Jerik agrees. "I can't even tell where the main metropolis starts and the outlying area ends."

"Definitely wasn't a large met," Seera says. "Probably no skyscrapers, but definitely a few big buildings."

"What big buildings?" Yaro asks, his thoughts coming across as amused.

"See that row of buildings right in the middle of the skyline?" Seera asks, and sure enough, there are four buildings with jagged angles. "Those were definitely twice the size before we got here."

"Pokkin' death from the sky," Kaed says.

"Hayu, brother," Yaro answers. "Mercy is weakness."

"That's our motto, Yaro, not AstroFor," Seera says. "Just for that, you're takin' lead."

"Hayu, Foreman," Yaro responds without objection, and we all follow behind him, making our way across the field and toward the battle.

***

Even with the enhanced capabilities of our attilas, it still takes us half an hour to get across the field. Once we get to the edge of the town, we find there's no ideal way to enter. We have to either dredge our way through swampland or climb up onto a major roadway.

"Well, I think it's obvious," says Kaed. "We take the road."

"I agree," Jerik says, his attila's head shaking. "It's gonna take us another half hour to march through that muck if none of us get stuck."

"Too bad this isn't a democracy," Seera says, looking back and forth between the road and the swamp. After a moment of silence, she looks back at the road, which is elevated several meters off the ground; easy for an attila to jump. "Aster," Seera breaks her silence. "Put a fusion round-up on the road. In between those loadbearing pillars."

"Foreman?" Aster asks.

"Just do it, Trooper!" Seera snaps.

"Hayu, Foreman," Aster answers, sounding defeated. She aims her fusion compressor and pulls the trigger once. The side of the roadway bursts, with concrete flying out in all directions.

"That's perfect, Amazon," Seera says, using the term female troopers like to call one another. "Hit it right there again."

Aster fires another shot, and this time the road gives. That entire section of roadway collapses, creating a makeshift ramp."

"That's what I'm talkin' about," Seera says, and I know that was meant to be a personal thought. "Kal, take the lead. Up the ramp!"

"Hayu, Foreman!" I say, grabbing my rifle and making my way to the collapsed road.

Before making my way up the ramp, I turn back to make sure my team is all with me, and they are, with Yeoman Jerik immediately behind me. As I emerge at the top of the roadway, I keep my rifle at the ready but see no obvious targets. The road is littered with abandoned vehicles, the kind that run off of fossil fuels. Type 1s love their fossil fuels. These vehicles also provide plenty of hiding spaces. The trick is to let my teammates clear the vehicles while I scout ahead where larger enemy forces may be positioned.

As I'm walking down the road, I notice there are lots of items strewn all over the place. Most of these items are bags, and I assume these bags contain nonessential items. There are also pieces of clothing and what appear to be children's toys.

"Civ-pop evacked," Kaed says, heavily using trooper slang. He means the civilian population evacuated already.

"Stands to reason," Seera says. "Looks like they got spooked and ditched the shit they didn't need."

We continue down the road for another ten minutes or so before Seera calls me back and orders Jerik to take the lead. The town becomes a tightly packed suburb, with what appears to be duplex houses lined up on both sides of the street, each occupying about a half-acre of land.

"We should clear these structures, Foreman," Jerik says, turning to face her.

Seera doesn't get a thought out before the ratatat tat of machine gun fire starts to light us up. Our shields glisten gold from close contact with the projectiles, but it's clear the angels aren't sure what they're shooting at. At least, not at first. Once our shields glisten, the machine guns zero in on our position.

"Get to cover!" Seera's thought comes off as frantic. "Where the pok is that coming from?"

"I got muzzle flashes!" Yaro answers. "3 o'clock!"

I move behind a vehicle in the closest driveway and peek through the window. Yaro is referring to our collective 3 o'clock, meaning slightly to the right of where we were heading. Sure enough, there are muzzle flashes coming from the second floor of one of the duplexes.

"Easy kill," Seera says. "Aster, take 'em out!"

There's no thought response from Aster, but I continue

watching the muzzle flashes until the entire side of the structure explodes.

"Pok yeah!" Kaed cheers.

"Nice shot, Trooper!" Jerik says.

"Yaro, Kal, clear that building!" Seera barks.

Yaro and I advance across the small suburban lawns. He makes it to the front door first, throwing his attila's weight against it and caving it in. I'm in close behind him. Yaro is proceeding forward down a hallway, and I look up the staircase where the machine gunner was. There's debris completely covering the staircase. If any angels are still up there, then they have nowhere but the windows facing our team to escape from.

I clear to the left, where there are several living areas with tables and couches and what appear to be entertainment centers set up.

"I got nothin'," I say.

"Clear here, too," Yaro says. "Got a basement over here. Watch my back!"

"Hayu!" I reply.

Yaro's standing, so his attila is aiming his stinger rifle down the basement stairs. I tap his shoulder, so he knows he's clear to descend. As he starts to go down, I turn to cover our backs. Just as I do, I see an angel come from the back door. This particular species of angel is quite humanoid. It stands on two plantigrade legs and has two arms. Its face doesn't look human at all, though. Not that I would have expected it to. It's wearing digitized camouflage and carrying a long gun of some kind. None of its gear strikes me as professional military. Before it even realizes it's in danger, I lift my stinger and put two rounds into it.

"Angel down," I say to let Yaro know there's no threat.

We continue down to the basement and clear it.

"Yaro, Kal," It's Seera. "Get your asses back out here. We have more contacts!"

Sounds from the outside world don't get picked up on thought comms. Only what we're thinking goes out. I can, however, hear the report of guns coming from outside the structure.

We make our way back up to the ground level and head for the front door, where we had made entry. Before we exit, I take a knee at one of the windows to see what the situation looks like outside. The rest of our team hasn't moved. I look to the right, down the street toward the heart of the city. There are angels shooting at our team from several houses on the opposite side of the street, and I can hear stinger fire coming from our side of the street as well.

I aim my stinger at one of the windows across the street and wait to see a muzzle flash. Once I see them, I pop off several rounds. The muzzle flashes don't start up again. Then I turn to the next window I had seen fire coming from and repeat the process.

There are several loud smacks, like a hammer striking bare wood, and holes appear in the wall next to me.

"Down, Kal, you're takin' fire," Yaro says, so I duck below the window.

More stingers pierce through the wall, bouncing off my

primary shield.

"Kal, Yaro." It's Foreman Seera. "Change of plans. Exit your building from the rear, and proceed two structures down. We're taking a lot of fire from that building. Take 'em out, and we'll clear the left side of the street. Hayu?"

"Hayu, Foreman!" Yaro and I respond.

"On me, K-junior," Yaro says.

I follow Yaro back through the building, passing the angel I had killed earlier as we exit out the back. We try to stay as quiet as possible. The angels have been having some difficulty seeing us, so our cam fields definitely conceal us from them, but it's only effective for sneaking up on them if we're quiet.

They, on the other hand, are not quiet. The closer we get to the duplex, the easier it is to make out the angels screeching back and forth to each other. Obviously, we have no idea what they're saying, but it gives us a pretty good idea of where in the house they are.

"Kal," Yaro says, pulling a frag grenade from his waist. "Through the second-floor window."

I nod, pulling a frag from my waist as well. We both activate the 'nades, and cook them for two seconds, then toss them through the window. There's a panicked screech just before they burst, and the volume of fire coming from the building drops by half.

Yaro is already kicking in the back door, and I rush to move in with him. He moves to the right, and I move forward down the hallway. An angel appears in front of me, and I raise my rifle.

Before I pull the trigger, I see it squint at me. As I move closer, its eyes grow wide, and it raises its own rifle. I put two rounds into it before it can even aim its weapon.

There's screeching coming from the right. If this duplex is identical to the other duplex we cleared, then this should be another living area, with the stairs to the second level on the left. I turn the corner and literally knock into an angel. The force of our collision is hard enough that it sends the angel crashing to the floor. I take one look at this angel and see it's wearing different combat gear than the other angel I killed. They don't have standardized gear. From what I learned in training about angel behavior, I'd say we're dealing with a civilian militia.

I put a single round into the angel's face before it can figure out what happened.

"How you holdin' up, K-junior?" Yaro asks, just as I hear the popping of relativistic projectiles coming from the basement.

"Building's hot," I answer. "Heading to the second floor."

"Yeah, I copy," Yaro says. "Be right with you. Basement's clear!"

I start to ascend the stairs and see two angels appear at the top. I aim my stinger and switch it to fully automatic fire, pulling and holding down the trigger. The two angels collapse down the stairs, coming to a halt as they smack against my attila's legs. I straddle over them and continue up the stairs, hearing the rapid footfalls of an angel coming closer and closer. I look up and see another angel coming at me. It slips on the blood from its two comrades and crashes head-first down the stairs. Its head smacks against the wall, leaving a hole in whatever feeble material is there, and it continues downward. Once again, my attila's legs stop the fall, but I grab the angel's head and twist.

"Ha!" Yaro says, and I can hear his attila coming up the stairs behind me. "Mercy is weakness, brother!"

The machine gun is firing as furiously as it was before. Whoever the angel is behind the trigger, they either never got the message that hostiles are inside the house, or they don't care.

I proceed forward across the hall from the top of the staircase, entering the room where the machine gun sounds like it's located. As soon as I enter, there's a loud bang, and my primary shield drops to the secondary. There are three distinctive pops from Yaro's stinger, and I hear a body hit the floor next to me.

"Shotgun guy is down. Take out the MG, Kal!" Yaro says.

The machine gunner turns away from the gun and towards the doorway. It doesn't have time to do anything before I put two rounds into it. I run up to the window, looking out over the street, and see our team moving across the street to clear the left side. It doesn't take long before I start getting shot at from those houses as well.

I drop back, my secondary shield quivering from contact.

"Take a second, brother," Yaro says. "Let your shield recharge."

"Thanks," I say, sitting down on the ground and looking over at the dead machine gunner.

The machine gunner isn't in military gear at all. They're in obvious civilian clothing: canvas pants, and some kind of material I'm not familiar with for the shirt. Black. I look up at the individual who had shot me point blank with a shotgun, and they, too, are wearing non-military clothing.

"Hey, Yaro," I say.

"Yeah?"

"These are unspecified targets." I point out, using the term we have for non-military angels.

"Yup."

"The angels on the stairs unspecified too?" I ask. "I didn't notice."

"That one you got with your hand was." Yaro laughs.

"Pok." I curse.

"Welcome to the Terrestrial Shock Troop Corps, bitch!" Yaro says.

***

We spend the rest of the day clearing buildings just like that. Two of us would clear a particularly problematic structure, and the rest of us would move up. The deeper into the city we went, the more military we found. Not that we didn't have our fair share of unspecified targets to neutralize, but at least we stopped feeling like a death squad and more like warriors. Needless to say, by the end of the day, we were all ready for a drink.

***

The first thing I smell is piss, but that's not unusual. Our physical bodies spend so long inside those attila links, we can't help but piss all over ourselves eventually. Luckily, the amphetamines they pump into us while we're in there tend to constipate us, so at least we're not covered in shit. Just piss.

The second smell is my own body odor. Musky and disgusting. The environment inside those attila links isn't exactly controlled by anything except our own body heat. It gets hot, and our bodies sweat. There's a reason the showers are a popular spot at the end of a shift.

I sit up in my link and immediately stand and stretch. "Pok," I say involuntarily as I get dizzy and have to sit back down.

"Worlds beyond, that was a day," Aster says, and I look over to see her grinning like a little kid who was just given a present.

"Yeah, it was. We really pokked them up!" I say with a laugh.

Yaro laughs, walking by my link and holding out his hand, which I take. "Good job today, brother. We made a good team out there."

"Yeah, we did!" I slap Yaro against the arm before he walks away.

"Yeah," Seera says with a tone that sounds like she's mocking us for being dense. "We really showed them not to mess with us."

I frown at her and look over at Jerik. He frowns back at me and shakes his head.

"Everything alright, Foreman?" I ask.

"Fine," she says, getting up from her link without meeting anyone's eyes. "Just need a shower and a drink."

As Seera walks off, I look back at Jerik. He gives me a look like I'm an idiot for saying something.

***

About an hour and a half later, I've showered, gotten my evening MRE pill, and I'm ready to unwind with a few drinks. The bar on our transport is identical to every other bar on a shock troop transport: stainless steel tables and chairs, with dim lights, so you don't notice the floors are stained from puke and blood.

I walk straight to the bar. That's always priority number one. I can find my teammates afterward.

"What can I get ya?" the bartender asks me.

"Uhh," I hesitate, looking at what's around. I'm new to drinking, so I haven't developed a preference yet. "What do you recommend?"

The bartender laughs. It's probably been several decades since our last deployment, so this is my first time meeting this bartender, who probably wasn't even alive when I last had a drink.

"Newbie, huh?" he asks. "Well, I guess it depends on what you're going for. You lookin' to get drunk or just relax?"

"I guess a little of both?"

"Hang on," he says, grabbing a bottle with a clear liquid and pouring some into a cup of ice. He then tops it off with what appears to be sparkling water. "There ya go, kid. Vodka tonic. You wanna try something with a little more flavor, come back, and I'll make a gin and tonic."

"Thanks," I say, handing him my cred card. He rings me up and hands it back.

Time to find my team. I don't see them anywhere. However, upon scanning the room, I see that Foreman Seera is off in a corner sitting by herself.

I walk over to the table and set my drink down. "Hey, Foreman. Can I join ya?"

She gestures to the chair across from her without speaking a word, and I sit.

"Couldn't see the rest of the team," I explain. "Didn't feel like going on a hunt."

"I think Yaro convinced Aster and Kaed to go to the cannaclub instead," she says, picking up her drink. "Something about the brothels being more fun."

I laugh. "That sounds about right."

I pick up my drink and take a sip. It's awful. I don't want to waste it, so I pinch my nose and slam it back, belching afterward in an attempt to keep from vomiting.

Seera frowns at me. "What the pok was that?"

"Guy said it was a vodka tonic?" I say, putting the glass back down. "Tastes like shit, but I didn't wanna waste it."

"Worlds beyond, you cribbies are somethin' else these days."

"Foreman?"

"Nothin'." She shakes her head, taking a sip of her drink.

"Can I ask you a question, Foreman?"

"Okay . . ."

"What did you mean earlier? When you said we really showed them not to pok with us? The angels, that is."

"Nothing," Seera says, looking away and taking another sip of her drink. "I was in a bad mood."

"C'mon, Foreman. You meant something by that, and I wanna know."

Seera looks at me like she wants to rip my head off. "You do understand that I outrank you, right?"

"Yes," I say, not understanding the relevance.

"You also understand that you're still the pokkin' new guy, right?"

"Yeah," I say, leaning in. "So, make me understand why a textbook deployment put you in a bad mood."

Seera smirks, but it's a joyless smirk. "You got balls, kid. I'll give you that."

"Thanks?"

"Okay." Seera leans in. "Here's the deal: today we killed a lot of people. People who just wanted to live their lives in peace, and we took all that away from them. Permanently."

"People?" I say, not exactly interrupting Seera but not letting her finish, either.

"Yes, people," she replies.

"Foreman, angels aren't people . . ."

Seera lets out a condescending laugh. "Is that what they told you in Indoc? We're killing savage beasts so that our proud and noble civilization can thrive?"

"Aren't we?"

Seera leans back in her chair and stares at me for a moment, never breaking eye contact. "You're a cribbie, Kal. And you're brand new to the Fleet. Eventually, you're going to understand this for yourself. These 'angels' are intelligent lifeforms, just like us. Their only crime is not being more advanced than us. Every single angel we killed today had hopes and dreams, and probably even people they loved. Many of them would have probably been thrilled to make peaceful first contact with us. But that's not what we do. The Gliesie Republic. The Terrestrial Shock Troop Corps. We don't do peace."

I just sit there, looking at my hands.

"You listenin' to me, Trooper?" Seera asks, kicking me under the table.

"Yes, Foreman," I answer.

"And? Is your world crumbling down around you? Or do you understand why they feed you that bullshit propaganda?"

"I understand, Foreman," I answer.

"Do ya?" Seera asks, picking up her drink and slamming it back. "I'm turning in for the night. We'll probably get deployed again tomorrow, and one of us should be well rested."

"Hayu, Foreman," I say, allowing myself a weak chuckle.

Seera stands up and starts to walk away, but she pauses and places a hand on my shoulder. "Don't think too hard about what I said, kid. Better to not think at all in this life."

She doesn't wait for me to respond before walking away.

I don't need to think about it. I understand what she's saying completely. I just happen to disagree with her. Not only that, I think what she's saying is incredibly dangerous. Foremen in the TSTC shouldn't hold these opinions, nor should they feel comfortable sharing them with their subordinates.

I debate what I want to do. I could get another drink, or I could meet up with the rest of my team at the cannaclub. They may have already sauntered off to the brothel, though. I tried cannabis last reanimation, and I didn't like it very much. Made me feel paranoid. I'm also not feeling particularly horny, not after that conversation with Seera.

That makes my decision for me.

I leave the bar and walk the halls of our troop transport, mostly empty now, with all of my fellow shock troops out partying, forgetting that their lives consist of nothing more than going into cryo, waking up, and killing. They may have been destined to rot away in prison or out on the streets, but this isn't much better. There are times where the Fleet feels like its own prison, and I've only been around for two reanimations.

By the time I get to the showers, I'm feeling the drink I had. I'm not feeling drunk but definitely relaxed enough to make what I have to do more tolerable.

I find the fifth stall from the left and open the door. I access the jumpsuit distributor and enter my shock troop credentials. It gives me a fresh jumpsuit in my size and with my name and team number on them. I strip down and enter the shower, turning it on. Freezing cold, as to be expected. But I had already showered. This is just my excuse to be in here.

I go to the far wall and find the fourth tile up from the floor and eighth from the left. Then I tap: twice on the upper right corner of the tile, once on the bottom right, three times on the upper left, and then twice more on the bottom right. That's my access code. A small sliver of the tile ejects from the wall, just enough for me to remove the rest manually. The screen automatically boots up to a simple readout, and I enter my message:

Ólimpis møst fol

Lusifyr haz folin frøm greïs

It's Shadow Operative code. I don't understand the references, but Olympus must fall means the foreman of my team is the subject, and the subject must be neutralized. Lucifer has fallen from grace means that the subject has become an angel sympathizer.

I place the transponder back into its secret port, and it seals back up. Even I, a trained Ghost, can't even tell it's there. I just know that my transponder is there because that's what I was told during my pre-insertion briefing.

I continue with my shower, deciding to go to bed after this.

Seera was right. We'll probably be deployed again tomorrow, and probably the day after that, and the day after that. No more than a couple of months of deployments. None of that really matters for me. What matters is: will I be the one to kill Seera, or will they take care of it? Only time will tell. It'll probably take some time for word to get back to command. If I wake up next reanimation and Seera is dead, then I'm off the hook. But if she's alive and doesn't die within the following 50 hours, I'll have to handle it. That's a prospect I'm not in favor of. But I'm a Shadow Operative. We're resourceful.

GRAMPY
BY JOSH SPICER

"We are leaving, Tim! Behave for your grandfather, and we will see you tomorrow," his mother cheerfully called upstairs. Her smile started to twist as she turned toward her father-in-law.

"I know what you are going to say, Melissa," growled Charles. "You can't control me no matter what you say."

"Fucking shit, Charles," Melissa groaned, pinching her fingers on the bridge of the nose. "Your stupid tales always scare him, and you know that! I do not understand--" Light rustling came from upstairs, and Tim's door creaked softly.

"I do not understand why," she continued, lowering her voice to a hiss. "Why do you want to scare your own grandson? He is literally 8, and you give him enough nightmares to send an adult to a mental asylum. If I come home and he has a hint of fear in his eyes, you will go straight into a home, and Mike will not be able to change my mind this time." Her heels clicked on the wooden floorboards as she strutted angrily towards the door.

"I was always right about you," Charles mumbled. Why did he ever let his son marry that witch? Whatever. She was his problem now.

Charles groaned as he started to walk up the stairs. His wife nagged him about getting one of those stair lifts, but those were for the inept. He was only 72. I am not dead yet, thought Charles, gritting his teeth as his knee started to pulse with pain. He was no wimp; he would make it eventually. Pain was the least of his problems. He had to have an important conversation with his precious grandson.

***

Tim rolled over, then rolled over the other way in frustration. How was he supposed to sleep without a bedtime story? Mum always reads a story. He loved when she would read books about planes, describing how they dipped and dived through the sky like a spaceship. His trip to Disney with his parents was amazing, but not because of the destination; Tim tolerated rides and enjoyed the occasional ice cream cone. He thought the space rides were great and hid from the creepy mouse mascots. What made his heart skip a beat, though, was pressing his face against the glass and watching the clouds glide by the huge wings cutting the wind. Ever since, he has taken out a book on airplanes every week from their public library. After months of this, the librarian smiled at his gleaming face, his little hands holding up the thick airplane encyclopedia above his head, and let him keep it.

Since Mum went out with Dad tonight, he did not know what Grampy would read. He never read him any books but seemed to be like a book himself. His eyes would glaze over as he would begin telling long tales of different times, different places, and different people to Tim, who wrapped himself in a blanket cocoon. Tim loved the stories with birds soaring over the trees and knights charging into battle for the love of princesses. However, some stories he would tell weren't about birds or knights or castles or princesses. Some stories were creepy, wrong, off, and almost too real. Some stories made the little white hairs on his skin rise from their slumber, standing straight up like resurrected cadavers. Some stories made him more awake than he had ever been before. Tim really hated these stories, but Grampy always would say, "I'm sorry if I scared ya, Tim my boy, but some stories need to be told." Tim didn't understand why they had to be told, but all he knew was that the world could be really scary.

As he lay in bed restlessly, he heard the pitter-patter of paws walking by his door and a gentle "meow." I thought Whiskers was already upstairs, Tim thought. I guess he must have gone down to look out the bay window, where he can look into the backyard and the surrounding woods. Grampy always told him that animals kept away what we fear, so maybe Whiskers was keeping the Boogie Man at bay. Thanks, Whiskers!

Flickering orange light flooded into his room as the door creaked open. Tim instinctively pulled the covers up over his head (like that would really save him from anything), but the outline of Grampy put him at ease.

"Hey, Tim my boy, you asleep?" Grampy's gruff whisper shredded through the still silence of Tim's bedroom.

"I'm awake, Grampy," Tim said in a small, cautious voice.

"Great. I got a story to tell ya. Wanna hear it?"

Something about Grampy's voice made Tim feel a bit on edge.

He may be young, but he could sense Grampy's forced excitement and fake enthusiasm. Something hid between his words that Tim couldn't figure out what that something was. Maybe he didn't want to know.

"Is it about planes? Or flying?" questioned Tim, sounding almost desperate.

"Another time, lad, maybe another time," Grampy said flatly. "This story does not have to do with planes or flying for that matter. This story is important for you to know. I want you to remember this story, okay? You have to listen carefully."

"Okay, Grampy," Tim said formulaically. He wished this was about flying or something normal. The night was already a bit too quiet.

Grampy shuffled into his room, swearing under his breath as he maneuvered over stray Lego blocks, Nerf bullets, and dirty soccer shorts. Slowly leaned himself down onto a wooden stool in the corner of Tim's room. He held his bad knee, trying to massage it. Ever since he fell, walking has even made him grimace at times.

"Are you ready, big guy?

"I guess so," Tim murmured quietly.

Charles paused, contemplating how to make the story digestible for an 8-year-old. Finally, he closed his eyes and began the tale:

"Let's begin. Once upon a time... uhh... Charlie lived a relatively normal life. He had a job, started a family, bought a house... you know, normal adult stuff. But one thing that is inevitable, Tim, is that there will be people who don't like you, no matter how good of a person you become. There will be those who call you names, make fun of you, maybe even give ya the one-two a few times, but those people will come and go. They are not who I'm talking about. Charlie had enemies who wanted to do really, really mean things to him. Charlie foolishly promised a woman his love in a moment of weakness, but he loved another woman. Truthfully, he was afraid to tell the woman he loved someone else, but if he told her earlier, he would not have fallen into the mess he got himself into--"

"Grampa?"

"Yeah?"

"Um... why would he be with a girl he didn't love?"

"Well... ugh... you will learn when you are older, but all I know is that he should have never gone to her in the first place and just stayed loyal to the one he loved. Anyway, as he tried to get away from the woman he didn't love, she became more attached and angrier. She felt that he belonged with her. Belonged to her. Charlie was starting to get nervous because he did not want the two women to meet, so----" Charles looked at his hands. "He made her disappear so she never would bother him and his perfect, new life."

"How did he get her to disappear?"

"I can't tell ya that one or your mum would not let me see you anymore. Charlie made her disappear, but she...uh...um wasn't where he left her. He was positive that he got rid of her forever, but she somehow...got away. Charlie thought that was strange, but he didn't want to think about it anymore and went on with his life. As days went by, Charlie started to realize that something wasn't right. He started to see...weird things. He would see two of the same person at times, which was creepy in itself. But the worst part about these strange moments was that one of the two clones was always, ALWAYS, staring straight at him. No matter what public space he was in, the one clone would not take its eyes off of him. As time went on, this thing would appear more and more in his life. Sometimes, he would be at the market or at a ball game, and he could feel their eyes burning into his back. Was he a bit paranoid? Maybe. Probably. But all he knew was that those clones who stared at him always had her eyes. The eyes of someone whose eyes should not have life in them. Tim, I tell you this story for a specific reason. What has been happening...happened to Charlie is partly his fault, but there was no turning back. This is his life now, and he needs to be aware and protect the people he loves. If you ever see two of the same people, you need to tell me, okay?"

"Okay, Grampy."

"I will be in your parent's room if you need me," Charles grunted loudly as he got up to leave.

"Grampy?"

"Yeah Tim?"

"Did you know Charlie?"

There was a brief silence, then Charles answered, "You could say that. Goodnight Tim. Be safe for me."

Tim heard shuffling as Grampy's limping self exited the room and watched the rectangular light shrink until all Tim could see was black. Tim kept thinking of Charlie and his strange dilemma. How did he see two of the same people? Tim had only seen that once, and they were twins that were in his kindergarten class. He hated them since they always would try to dismantle his glorious Lego masterpieces. Grampy also said that he himself had to be careful, but what did he have to do with it? He had never met this Charlie guy or even known a Charlie. He wondered if Mum would know Charlie. He'd ask in the morning at breakfast. As these thoughts streamed through Tim's mind, cracks of light filled the room as his door slowly creaked open.

There was a silence that seemed to go on forever. The world to Tim seemed so small at that moment; There was just him, a person's silhouette, his room, and silence. After what seemed like a million minutes, Tim heard Grampy whisper,

"Tim, buddy? Are you awake?"

Tim sighed again with relief. "Yes, Grampy."

"Were you talking to someone?"

Tim lay confused. What was he talking about?

"No, just you."

"What?" Grampy hissed.

"Just you, Grampy."

There was a long pause. Grampy's voice was low but stern. "Come with me right now. Don't ask questions. We need to get out of here."

Tim got out of bed, a bit confused. Then it all clicked. He felt his blood rush out of his body. If this was Grampy, who was he talking with?

He hurried behind Grampy, who ran quickly down the stairs, and they both bolted out of the house. Grampy opened the door to the car and ushered Tim inside, and buckled him in. Grampy jumped in the driver's seat and skidded out of the driveway, gravel shooting up in the air. Tim peered behind them out the back window. He saw lights turn on in the house and a shadow limp across the 2nd-floor window.

They drove quickly through their small town square and skirted onto the nearest highway. As they drove at a more consistent speed, Tim calmed down and collected his thoughts. His eyes darted back and forth, and his brow creased in thought. His voice wavered as he looked at Grampy.

"Uh, Grampy?"

"Yes, Tim?"

"Mum said you hurt your knee really badly. How did you run down the stairs so fast?"

IN THE TOWN OF ABERMOURE
By Kia Jones

The allure of small-town life hits differently when your body is condemned to a life of misery. Live out the last of my days in a hospital or in a quiet town with no bills and no responsibilities? I guess you could say I definitely took the ladder. Ambermoure offered itself as my new home when the Mayor of the town made an appeal for workers.

'Our beautiful town could prosper if we only had a dozen extra people to help us,' she said in her broadcast to the surrounding areas and cities. 'Which is why I'm offering free housing to anyone who answers this call, saying they are the best at what they do. Whatever it may be that you can offer me, I will put you to work in Ambermoure, and you will never have to pay for the pillow under your head or the food in your stomach.'

Why not, eh? I could bartend like it was nobody's business back in Jersey. The nighttime life was second to none, and I stood at the pinnacle of it all in the best bar around.

Besides, when the end of your road is just around the corner, it seems useless to have a job and make money but even more useless to pay rent for another month when I may not even last that long. At least this way, I could have a little bit of money to leave to my brother back home in Jersey.

"You seem absolutely drowned in your thoughts." A voice came from the other side of the bar. I turned to face him, his sudden appearance making me jump.

"Sorry about that." I set my towel down. I had been mindlessly polishing a glass. "What can I get for you?"

"Bourbon. Leave the bottle," he said with a wink.

"Oof, life getting you down, too?" I prepped a short glass with two round ice cubes and pulled the bourbon out from the shelf behind me.

"You could say that." He tapped the bar top with his finger.

"I'm all ears if you need." I poured the liquid into his glass. He raised the glass to an unheard toast, then threw back the drink in one swig.

"I'll tell you mine if you tell me yours." He set the glass back down. I refilled it, then set it back down closer to him.

"I don't know about that. It's a tall price to pay nowadays to know my secret."

"Convicted felon?" he guessed.

"No. Not yet, anyway." I laughed.

His eyebrow raised as he took a sip. "Well, now you've got me increasingly intrigued. Are you secretly a serial killer here to murder the remaining population of Ambermoure?"

I chuckled at his antics. I had been here nearly a week, and this was my first time to see his face. His short black hair was swept back with a gel, and his sage green eyes glimmered with mischief.

"What about yourself? You're not the type to be the town menace, are you?"

"Oh no, not at all." He said with a wink, taking another sip. He sat in silence for a minute. Waiting, I assume, for me to tell him 'my secret.'

"Trust me," I began. "You're better off not knowing."

"Usually, bartenders are a bit more open to story time," he teased. I could hear the lilt in his voice, though his serious gaze tried to hide it.

"That's because the town drunk is usually the one spilling the beans, and the bartender clocks out with a wad of cash."

"So what you're saying is I can pay you to talk to me?"

"If you've got the balls to admit that the only way you'll get a woman's attention is by paying her, then, by all means, cough up the bills."

"That's not the only way." His voice dropped into an alluring whisper.

I leaned in, matching the volume in his voice. "Talking to women after you've drunk fucked isn't a valid reason for bragging rights either." I winked.

He finished his glass in silence for a second, unsure how he ended up in a hole that required digging. "Let me try this again." He cleared his throat. "I'm Sage Deamonté," he said, holding out his hand.

"Nice to meet you, Mr. Deamonté. I'm Livia." I took his hand firmly.

"Oh, please, for the love of god, call me Sage. Deamonté is far too formal, especially in a town like this," he requested.

"Sage, then. That's a beautiful name."

"Thank you, it really brings out my eyes, doesn't it?" He fluttered his lashes.

I couldn't help but laugh, covering my mouth to try to hide it. The comment threw me off guard, and I shook my head. The grin on his lips said unbridled pride at my reaction to his joke.

"Alright, alright, you got me," I admitted.

"That was pretty good, wasn't it?"

I shook my head, giving him only a moment to revel in his pride and moving on from the teasing banter. "Do you live here? I've not seen you before," I asked.

"I was thinking the same thing about you. I grew up here. I was away for a bit with work, though."

"I just got here a week ago. I saw your mayor offering free housing in exchange for help."

"What a pathetic excuse for a cry for help disguised as a call to action." He shook his head; his tone held a sudden and almost frightening disgust as he poured another glass of bourbon.

"You don't agree with her methods?" I raised a brow.

"Not in the slightest." He set the bottle down a little harder than I think he intended.

"Well, it brought me here. And one other person that I know of."

"Probably because you're too poor to afford anything else," he muttered after a long swig of his drink.

I paused. "Ouch. And it was going so well. Why don't you, uh…finish your rich man drink in peace." I shot back, leaving my spot behind the bar. My shift was almost done anyway. I could blame it on not feeling well if the owner asked why I was leaving already.

I heard Deamonté call out to me once, but I didn't even turn. He didn't deserve even a moment of hesitation for that crack.

The weekend brought about a town holiday called Sacrosanct Parade. Nothing was open except for the hospital and one small convenience store. I only knew that little tidbit because I was in the hospital most of the day. When I was released, I walked for about 30 minutes before I finally found something open that sold food. I bought a few snacks from that convenience store, and when I left, I realized all the hubbub that was happening in the town square. It was filled with people, and many of them were bringing food. Some of them were dressed in period-accurate outfits, and they looked absolutely miserable in the summer heat.

I crossed the street to the square, trying to understand what was happening that caused places to close down for the day. 'Sacrosanct Parade,' a sign read.

"You stick out like a sore thumb." A voice came from behind me. I spun around to see Sage standing tall in a custom-tailored suit. I hadn't seen him at the bar since the night we first met a few days ago. Another man stood with him, also dressed in a fancy, fine-tailored suit.

"I feel like a sore thumb. What is all this?" I asked.

"A parade and picnic held for the 1874 Act. The town celebrated when it was officially recognized as sacred land." He responded. Then, like an afterthought, "Oh, Livia, this is my brother, Darius Deamonté."

Darius Deamonté took a step forward, offering his hand. I reached out to shake it, but he, instead, lifted my fingers to his lips, kissing the top of my hand. "It's a pleasure to meet you," he said.

"Wow…you guys really get into this whole thing, don't you?"

"Well, our family holds this day in high esteem. It's kind of required that we get into it," Sage said.

"Our great-great-grandfather was one of the many people that made the bill of sacred land possible," Darius said, releasing my hand.

"Ah, so you are rich white men." I shot a glare at Sage, who only avoided my gaze and cleared his throat.

"Will you be staying for all the shenanigans?" he questioned.

"I don't know, am I allowed? Or would I happen to be too poor to join in on the founding family's fun?" I asked, still staring Sage down.

"I'm not sure what my brother has done to upset you," Darius began. "But, you are more than welcome to join us for the picnic. Please, allow me to escort you?"

I finally turned my eyes back to Darius. He was holding his hand out, and a genuine smile gently parted his lips.

"Sure," I sighed. "I've got nothing else going on today." I took Darius' hand, and he tucked it into the crook of his elbow, leading me off into the crowd.

"Careful, brother," Sage said, stepping up beside me and

placing my other hand in the crook of his elbow. "This one's got quite the bite on her." He winked down at me.

"Something you enjoy, I'm sure," I quipped.

"No surprise there." He smiled.

The two of them escorted me through the square, stopping at each attraction they deemed important. I got an entire history class worth of information in about 30 minutes of walking and talking. Darius was far nicer to talk with than Sage, but Sage continuously found ways to make me laugh and keep the long and droning history lessons entertaining.

"Let's take a short break," Sage said, offering an open picnic blanket to sit on.

I was grateful for the timing of his suggestion. Having been in the hospital all morning left me feeling drained. I hope he didn't see how tired I was.

"Darius, why don't you go grab some drinks and food," Sage suggested. He only sat down with me once his brother turned to leave. "Are you okay?"

Well, shit.

"Yeah, I'm good," I said, doing my best to cover up the pain on my face. It felt like a fire was burning my stomach from the inside.

"My brother has a love for history. You'll have to forgive his boring prose."

I forced a smile. "It's fine."

"So, listen, I've been meaning to say this, but I didn't want to do it in front of my brother." He cleared his throat. "What I said the other day, that was uncalled for. The mayor and I don't really see eye to eye and…well, either way, that's not your fault or your business, so I apologize for what I said."

"Wow…I'm impressed."

He hesitated for a moment, confusion on his face. "Please tell me what I just did so I may continue doing it." His blatant simping was both cute and laughable.

"You apologized. You didn't strike me as the kind of guy who could say 'I'm sorry.'"

"Oof. I deserve that."

"It's alright. Thank you for your apology." The pain flared up again, and I stiffened my back, trying to keep it under wraps.

"Are you sure you're alright?" he asked, placing a gentle hand on my shoulder.

"I'm fine. I've just been in the hospital all day."

"What happened?" He seemed genuinely concerned, leaning forward a bit to meet my eyes.

I swallowed back a lump in my throat. "Nothing out of the ordinary."

"You look in pain."

"Yeah, I kind of am." I grabbed my stomach. The pain was worse than cramps at the moment.

"Should I take you home?" he asked.

"Nope. Just give it a second. It'll go back to a dull roar soon enough."

"Are you sick?"

"You could say that," I groaned. He just stared at me, waiting for a better explanation. I looked around. There were people in earshot; I didn't want to talk about it here. He got the hint and stood, helping me up with him. We sat on a bench at the far end of the square.

"I'm pregnant..." I whispered. "But also, not really."

"What do you mean?" His gaze never left mine, both confusion and sorrow written on his brows.

"I got an abortion...but it's illegal in my home state."

A sudden understanding flashed through his gaze in the way his lips softened into a frown. "So you did it under the table..." he guessed.

"Yeah...I don't think I got it from a reliable source. I knew something was wrong right away, but I can't fix it. If I admit to it, I'll just be put in jail. And even if I admit to it now, it's not like anything can save my life. I've got human remains up there...nothing's passed yet like they said it would."

"What were you at the hospital for?" He asked.

"There's only one other person who knows what I did. She checked my uterus to see if she could help. She said I'd be alright, but I knew she was lying. It's fine, though." I forced a smile again. "I came here to die anyway."

"You shouldn't give up so easily." He gently reprimanded. "You have a whole life ahead of you."

"Not anymore. Honestly, it's okay, though. I won't have to live in this hell of a world anymore. Why would I change that now?" I laughed to try to fill the awkwardness with more sound.

"Because it's still your life. You shouldn't just let it get ripped away from you because that guy was an asshole."

The fake smile on my face flattened, and I couldn't stop myself from getting a wave of fear. "You're right. I shouldn't. But it has been, and I can't change that now."

He looked into the crowd. A furrow was heavy on his brow. Small beads of sweat glistened on his skin from the sunny afternoon. "I'm not even in your shoes, and I'm frustrated for you." He sighed. "This isn't fair."

"Life's not fair...besides, we were strangers just a few days ago. No point in shedding a tear for me now." I waved him off.

The pain hit again in a cold wave of chills. I heard him reply, but my brain was otherwise too occupied to understand what he said. I only vaguely heard myself whisper. "Oh shit," before I went down, the afterthought of the warm grass on my cheek as I slipped into blackness.

The warmth on my cheek remained even as I awoke. Though it took me a second to realize my surroundings, I soon recognized that the warmth was a ray of sunshine drifting into an otherwise darkly lit living room. The next thought to hit my foggy brain was that the pain in my stomach had subsided again. I sat up on the leather couch that I was lying on. My surroundings were completely unfamiliar. Wasn't I just at the town square with–?

"Good evening, sunshine," Sage said from across the room. I turned to see him coming in from another room, a glass of amber liquid in his hand.

"What happened?"

"You passed out. I brought you here."

"Where is here?"

"My home." He sat in an armchair across from me, placing the glass of liquor on the table beside it.

"What did you do to me?" I asked.

"Come now, do you really have that little faith in me?"

"No–no. I just mean my stomach isn't hurting. Did you give me some kind of medicine?" I placed my feet on the cold floor, only just realizing he had taken the time to remove my shoes and place a blanket over my shoulders.

"You could say that."

My throat tightened, and I had to swallow the pain of wanting to cry. "Please stop…" I whispered.

"What was that?" He put a hand to his ear. "Thank you, Sage." He mimicked a female voice. "Oh, you're welcome, Livia. It was–"

"Stop it!" I clenched my jaw. "Stop caring about me. You barely know me, okay? I don't need your sympathy."

"You don't need it, or you don't want it? Because from where I'm sitting, I see a woman who doesn't want to be in this mess. I can help–"

"I don't need it." I shot back through gritted teeth.

"That's a lie, and you know it." He kept his voice calm. It only infuriated me more that he remained so stoic.

"You don't know what I've been through. Don't pretend like

I'm a lost puppy that you can save."

"No, I don't know what you've been through. But I can see what you're living through, and I want to help if you'll just–"

"Just what? Admit that I'm the epitome of hopelessness? No. I won't–I ran away so I wouldn't have to feel that again; how it felt to have people look at me like I'm a lost cause. Only in death will I ever be free from it..." I paused to take a breath but that pause allowed for the tears to flow. "But then I'll never know how to live without it."

He sat quietly. It was frustrating to see that his eyes didn't really hold a helpless sympathy. Instead, they held kindness. The type of kindness that makes you feel like there's nothing wrong with the world because it's simple and honest kindness.

It made me angry. Angry that I found such relief from a stranger. But if I was so angry, then why did telling him the truth come so easily?

"I don't want to die," I whispered. "I left everything and everyone I've ever known, so I wouldn't have to admit that I don't want to die. I'm not tired of living. I'm just tired of living in a hospital. Tired of seeing the world behind a window."

Sage got out of his chair and, in humbleness that I've never experienced, got on his knees in front of me, a gentle hand on my cheek as he wiped away a tear that was quickly replaced by another.

"I came here to live out my days until I die," I continued. "But I don't want to regret my last few days. I just want to live." I met his gaze, "And to love. I don't want to die...I just didn't want to die with regrets. Turns out I might not have enough time for that."

"I need you to listen to me..." He whispered, his hand still holding my cheek. "I can help you. I can take all that pain away."

"Please don't give me false hope. Not even a doctor–"

He placed a finger over my lips. "Shh. Just listen, please." I shook my head. He brushed his thumb past my lips on his way to wipe another tear. "I'm a vampire." He said. "I gave you some of my blood to take that pain away, but I can fix your problem too."

"Wha–how?" I stuttered through my words, still processing what he was trying to tell me.

"If I bite you...turn you. If you let me turn you into a vampire, you will never have to experience this pain again."

"That's not possible."

"It is, I promise you. I swear to you, Livia, I am not lying. Trust me. Trust me, and I can end your suffering." When I still remained unable to answer, he took my hands, leading us both up to our feet. "I want you to live and experience your life the way you were meant to. You deserve that much and so much more. To live...to love," his fingers were at my cheek again, tracing the curve of my jaw, my lips, tucking hair behind my ear, and gently tracing down my neck.

"Why?" The simple question was all I could manage between the butterflies and the confusion.

"Are you incapable of believing that a chance at life is a basic right that you are entitled to? No matter the things that have happened to you?"

Tears burned my eyes as I thought about what he said. Being a woman sometimes feels like nothing more than being a prize. A toy. Even trash. "I just...I just wanted to exist as me. Not as a vessel for an unwanted child. And I wanted people to be okay with that."

"That is all I want for you. I want you to live as you are, and experience life as you should. Will you trust me?" He squeezed my hands. I looked down at my hands in his, confused and elated at what he was offering me.

"Will it hurt?"

"I promise you, you will feel nothing."

I lifted my hand to his face, a conviction tightening around my chest. "Sage Deamonté, please save me," I said with a fervent urgency.

"As you wish." His canines grew into fangs as he spoke, and a darkness overtook his eyes. Still, they remained as they were; kind.

He brushed my hair to the right side of my neck and leaned into my left ear. I felt his hot breath on my skin, and a shiver went down my spine. His lips pressed gently into the base of my neck, and the cold sensation of his teeth sunk into my flesh. I gasped in reaction to it but quickly realized he was right; I felt no pain. Only a warm tingle as he sucked at my neck.

My head started to spin, and I grabbed his arms at my waist to stay steady. I felt my head getting heavy, and I leaned on his shoulder, the world around me getting fuzzy and my eyes fluttering.

He pulled away from my neck and supported my head with his hand, whispering, "Let go and quietly pass. I will be here when you awaken once more."

I can tell you nothing of the time that passed while I was dead. It's funny. I thought I would have some eye-opening experience. Apparently, dying by a vampire bite means nothing to the universe since it's not a real death. The most I remember is floating in an abyss, feeling nothing at all. No pain, no fear. Hearing no thoughts, not even my breathing or heartbeat. It truly was a void and, oddly enough, it was a paradise.

"Livia?" I heard a disembodied voice in the darkness. A coldness washed through me like a sudden winter storm. Then I felt a hand on my arm, and my body shook.

"Livia. Wake up." The voice pleaded. But I fought it. If I woke up, that meant that I would have to go back to a reality of pain and grief.

My eyes snapped open unwillingly, and I gasped for air as if I had just been drowning. Arms were around me in seconds, my face buried in a chest.

"There you are. I was getting a bit worried. You had been out for hours," Sage said. He released me when I stopped squirming, my surroundings coming back to me. I was in Ambermoure. In Sage Daemonté's house. We had been talking and then he…he bit me. I lifted my hand to my neck. Two small holes remained though they were covered by dried blood.

"How do you feel?" he asked, sitting on the bed beside me.

Bed? I looked around the room. He had moved me to a bedroom while I was out. The bed was made with a thick and warm comforter that I currently sat under. Finally, I looked up at him.

"I don't feel anything," I muttered in disbelief.

"You're currently still in transition. You need blood to complete the process. But there's no pain anymore, right?"

I swallowed a lump in my throat. Tears welled up in my eyes. "It doesn't hurt anymore."

He smiled. "See? I told you I could help."

I put a hand on my stomach over my uterus and pressed. Where normally I felt a lump, was only soft flesh. "It got rid of everything?"

"Vampire blood heals anything. It can cure diseases, close up wounds. Even a botched-up abortion."

I smiled. "Thank you." I lifted the comforter off and swung my legs over the side of the bed, but before I could move any further, I froze. A life with no pain was so freeing that, for a moment, I was debilitated.

Sage extended his hand to me. I looked up at him. His piercing eyes held the same kindness I remembered from earlier. So he still looks at me the same way even when I'm not at death's door. I took his hand and got to my feet, stepping into a new life and new world all at the same time.

"Welcome to the town of Ambermoure, Livia. We'll have plenty of time to figure out where we're going next."

CASTAWAYS
By Stephen Faulkner

Star Child handles with the ease of a summer breeze. I have been going on now for what seems like an eternity, yet I know that it has been only a little more than a month in Earth time, and my fuel is running perilously low. I am an exile, having been set adrift with a negligible supply of food and fuel. I have no company save what my imagination can muster in its murmuring depths. Through the wisdom and totalitarian might of the High Council of Peers, I have been sentenced to traverse the heavens and to die a prolonged, dismal death of spirit and self in the confines of the infinity of space and my mind for my crimes against the State and its citizenry. My course was carefully programmed so that I would not come near any inhabited – or even uninhabited – planet. I would have no recourse but to hurtle through space like a powered meteor, going nowhere at great speed.

Though my craft has no official designation, besides a string of letters and numerals, I call her Star Child, and she handles like a zephyr breeze on a summer's languid afternoon, carrying me who-knows-where. I say "handles" even though I have no control whatsoever over her preordained course, which is a straight line that is now the arc of my destiny. I am no longer a man of Earth, for I have been disinherited by the mother-world that had nurtured me, the society that had fed me on its dreams and beliefs. I am now a man of the Universe, ever born into the solitude and fear of traveling through the naked void.

It is I, then, who should be called Star Child.

***

Weary, malnourished minds have wanted to play tricks on themselves, revealing solid realities that are not there. Mirage is what it is called, but I do not believe that that is what is happening unless part of the hallucination is the staunch belief that it is actually there, floating in the interstellar void like an indestructible balloon. It is a refueling station, or so it appears. Its three huge storage cylinders must contain more than enough of a supply to send a thousand vessels of Star Child's size packing with a full load of nuclear push-back into the cold depths of black nothingness.

It is true, I tell myself, and just in time, too, for my fuel gauges show that all of my craft's tanks of isotopic energy have been all but completely spent. A whisper in the ear, a murmur in the mind, tells me to rejoice at this eleventh-hour reprieve. And I do, but only for a scant moment, for then a remembered fact plunges me back into my well of deserved despair. The designers of Star Child have built my prison extremely well, for they have equipped her with an anti-gravity shield so that the little ship will repel and thusly bypass any close, solid objects. I shall bypass this one, as well, I keep telling myself, but the mammoth stations loom ever larger in my viewport, coming closer with each passing moment, beckoning like a mother to its babe. I am being drawn in by a force far greater than the push of Star Child's anti-grav field, and my plucky little vessel enters the station's narrow docking tunnel to land clumsily with a shuddering clunk that shakes my little home's thick bulkheads.

A large green light outside my viewport blinks spasmodically and then stays solidly lit. A sign nearby lights up, informing me of something in a series of blockish, alien characters. I check gauges that I never thought I would have the opportunity to use. Outside barometer reading shows an uncannily earthlike air pressure. The air composition is of nitrogen, oxygen, carbon dioxide, hydrogen, and trace elements; a little high in helium content but still very safe and very breathable. The temperature is 70 degrees, and the gravity is 98% that of Earth, so I will be about three pounds lighter here than I would be on my "home" planet.

I press the saucer-sized button that activates the door release. The floor panel quickly slides open, and a staircase drops quietly to the floor of the alien station's docking chamber. Air rushes in, and my lungs are suddenly filled with fresh, oxygen-rich gasses. I am dizzy for a moment but manage to hold my balance and exit Star Child, slowly at first but then with greater enthusiasm than I ever thought possible. My prison shackles have been broken; I feel I am a free man once again.

A tall man dressed in a red single-piece uniform waits for me at the far end of the docking chamber. He is olive-skinned, dark-haired, and he is smiling kindly. He says something in his language as he takes my arm to lead me away from my craft. I hold back, tell him in English, and with an abortive attempt at sign language that I do not understand what he is saying. He looks at me with a puzzled expression, then nods and walks a few steps away from me. He stops and, with a waving gesture, bids me to follow him. A door opens for us, sliding into the gray wall with a sucking sound. When it closes behind us, a second door opens before us, and we enter a room whose walls flicker and shine as if they are constructed of smoked glass, and the source of their rolling, shifting illumination is behind them. But it is the walls themselves that cast this very eerie glow. They are seamless, even at the corners, made of some phosphorescent material whose rippling patterns are quite beautiful and even rather mesmerizing.

My alien companion and guide directs me to the center of a black ring that is described on the floor, and he ducks into a side chamber of the little room. His soft voice comes over the intercom, peppered with static. Ush, dzom, tsel, raheth, pa.... The word "counting' comes to mind, for it seems that is what his words signify. It is all that I have time to think for at the word pa, my thoughts are no longer my own. In a nano-second, I am in the midst of a whirl of contradictory images and ideas; I feel woozy and about to black out. But the ordeal is soon over. The man returns from the side chamber, smiling once more.

"I am sorry for the misunderstanding," he says in his own tongue. I jump at the sound of his voice for though I understand his words as being foreign to my learning and ken, I can easily understand what he says without any difficulty whatsoever. The period of my discomfort, it seems, was all that was required for the waves generated by the glowing room to instill in my mind the basics of the language spoken by this man. "We get so few alien ships here and when we do, their occupants don't often bear such a striking resemblance to our own race as you do. I made the error of assuming that you were one of our own pilots. Please forgive my blunder."

"No apology is necessary," I say, then taste my tongue at the feeling of the strange words that my mouth is producing. "My name is James Erin."

The man takes my hand, and our fingers interlace in greeting. "I am Captain Talbor Karonn," he says. "Welcome to Fueling Station Shay-Kah 601."

***

Captain Karonn did some things rather oddly as far as my own social upbringing was concerned. One example of this was his serving a sweet dessert before the start of a sumptuous meal instead of at the end. On the whole, however, he showed off a strikingly aware and good-natured personality. The conversation which we held for more than an hour gradually turned to our respective origins. I told him that I was from the third planet, which was called Earth and which circled a middling-sized star at one extreme of a galaxy called the Milky Way.

The Captain muttered and mumbled his way through several mouthings of the names of the places I told him about and came up with something that sounded vaguely like "erith" and "micky aye" before he sighed and shook his head. "And where," he said in an unhidden attempt to change the subject. "Are you bound?"

"I don't know," I said before embarking on the story of how I got to be where I presently found myself. The Captain listened intently as I told him of the High Council of Peers, their tyrannical misuse of a basically sound judicial system, and how they and their immediate subordinates and the vast bureaucratic regime used the trusted system to suit their own ends. I then proceeded to tell of my part in a plot to kill one of the members of the Council and how we had so disastrously failed and were quickly tried and sentenced to a life of exile in spaceships whose controls were set on straight-line autopilot so that there would be no destination.

"So you see," I said, shrugging. "I've been traveling for more than thirty Earth days with no idea of my whereabouts or how far I've come from my home planet."

Karonn slapped his knee angrily and frowned. "I guess that puts you and me in rather the same position," he said.

"I don't think that I understand."

"Shay-Kah 601 has been off course for a little less than the time it takes my planet to make a full circuit of our sun," he explained. "All systems here are integrated, so when our gyroscopic guidance went out, we were completely unaware of it until we had drifted far enough off course that ships from our planet apparently could no longer find us. It is a stupid, wasteful thing, this being lost. We must be well outside our planet's shipping corridors, though, for us to lose all physical contact with home."

"But what about radio contact?" I inquired.

"We use an accelerated signal method this far out into deep space in order to cut down on response time between reception and transmission. That equipment went on the blink shortly after we had realized our positional predicament."

"And your last transmission from home couldn't help you get a fix on your position?"

"We were just about to get a line-fix on home when the equipment failed. Talk about bad luck. We can transmit, but we can't receive. If it had been the other way around, we could have gotten a fix on the direction from where the message from home had come and so made the necessary course changes and gotten ourselves back to where ships from our home planet could find us."

The Captain's face took on a pained though eloquent expression of resignation before our conversation lapsed into silence as deep as space. The conversation had thus come to an untimely end. I cast about in my mind for a logical continuation but only ended up asking how many people manned Shy Kah 601.

"Ten," he answered. "Five men and five women, including myself. "And talk about bad luck again. One of the women is pregnant."

"No commitment, either, I suppose," I said, using the corollary of this man's language for marriage, spouse, husband, life partner. He shook his head, and the conversation stalled once more.

Each of us sat nervously in one another's presence. There

should be so much more to say, curiosities about culture, life modes, and politics to satisfy, philosophies to share, but neither of us knew where to begin, did not seem to know what would or would not be deemed bad manners on the part of the other. Then, his mute reverie was suddenly broken by a thought that blazed in his watery, deep blue eyes.

"But we do have one thing that keeps up the morale of the crew, however," he said excitedly. "Besides sex, that is, and that is Jakor."

"Who?" I asked.

"It's not a who but a what. A sort of a sport. Come, I'll show you." Karonn bounced on his heels with the vibrant spirit of youth as he led me through the corridors of Shay Kah 601 to demonstrate to me the sport of his people called Jakor.

***

Opponents were pitted against one another, each armed with a six-foot-long pole. The young woman was dressed in a green jumpsuit and was clearly on the defensive, fending off and blocking numerous blows until she misjudged a side thrust and was struck on the arm by the tip of her opponent's pole. The point was called in favor of the young man with silvery gray hair.

"This is only an exercise, of course," said Karonn as we watched the match through a glass partition. "Jakor was originally a form of hand-to-hand combat used extensively in the armed services until the use of nuclear and trasoric weapons became the norm and the instances of war and international aggression became fewer and fewer until, at last, war is now only a word used in the history books. You see, on our planet, there are only three nations, and each has its own vast stockpile of nuclear and much more powerful trasoric armaments. So you can well imagine that any war would mean suicide for at least two if not all three of those powers. And so Jakor remains now only as a spectator sport, no longer used on the fields of battle."

"We had much the same situation on Earth several centuries ago," I said, surprised to find that there was, in his language, a word for century. "Mutually Assured Destruction was the term applied. The philosophy of deterrence was soon found to be sorely lacking. Luckily, other means were found to avoid such a devastating war; extensive negotiations were conducted which ultimately led to the formation of a world government and later, the High Council of Peers."

A lean man in a smartly tailored uniform approached us as we watched the Jakor match. He had deep-set eyes and a rigidly stern face and was introduced to me as Mariss Tork, Shak Kah 601's Jakor master.

"Mariss is a gold ring," Karonn informed me. "Only one step away from the highest honor of all Jakorizas, the therenium. Mariss, this is James Erin of the planet called Erith."

Mariss Tork's fingers interlaced with mine as we muttered our polite greetings to one another.

We sat and watched silently as the competition in pole work continued. The young man, whom I was told was a bronze ring, was winning four points to the one the young woman in the green jumpsuit had earned on a technical foul. It was a five-point match, and an ill-timed block of a downward thrust to the head of the woman gained the gray-haired man his winning point. As the woman walked out of the competition room, rubbing the sore lump at the back of her head Tork gave me some background on the players.

"The young woman, Seta, is only a beginner," he said. "There are five degrees of excellence in Jakor marked by the metal of which the wearer's ring is made – tin, bronze, silver, gold, and therenium. Seta, as a beginner, wears no ring and is working towards her tin and, I might add, doing very well, too. Talbor, our Captain here, is a bronze ring and getting so good that a silver is in the offing for him when we return home."

"If we ever do get home." Talbor Karonn bit his lip as he spoke. "Our friend, Mister Erin, here, knows as little of our position as we do, Mariss. I don't know if we will ever be returning home."

Tork quickly changed the subject to something less depressing. He asked if I had something akin to Jakor on my home planet. I replied in the affirmative and tried my best to explain with what little knowledge I possessed of Judo, Aikido, Karate, Kung Fu, and Ninjutsu. "It would seem that your Jakor is something of a subtle blending of Kung Fu and Karate with the skills of the Ninjutsu swordsman thrown in for exercise and the building of one's prowess and reflexes," I observed.

"Perhaps," said Mariss. "But there is more." Having said this, he held out his ring hand for my inspection. The ring was a wide, gold band on the middle finger of the left hand. There was writing etched into the metal around the circumference of the band and, on top, rising about an inch from the center like an animal's horn from the bone of the finger, was a sharp, conical point.

"If a man hit you in the right spot with this," said Tork. "You would double over in agonizing pain, and that would be the end of the fight, but I, with the correct application of the skills I have acquired, can direct a blow a few inches below your solar plexus, push my fist into your chest cavity –." He demonstrated the lethal method with a sharp, wrist-turning uppercut. "And tear the heart right out of your body in less time than it would take for you to draw your next breath."

"That was the way that a Jakor master was able to kill bare-handedly in time of war," Karonn explained. "As you can see, though, my ring has no kill point, as does Marriss'. Kill points are only allowed to gold and therenium ring wearers. Mine is only a bronze."

"Tradition only, of course," said Tork as we continued to watch the competitions on the other side of the thick glass. The gray-haired young man was now matched against a new opponent and was losing rather badly. "What's the real use of a kill point when there is no battle in which to put it to its intended purpose?

Oh look, Talbor, Kelam is making a true fool of poor Parlas."

"Kelam is a silver ring," Karonn told me. "Parlas is only a bronze, like myself. Even I would have a hard time with Kelam. Tork, however, being a gold, would be able to handle both of them, Kelam and Parlas, at the same time, single-handedly."

"Perhaps,' said Tork in a gruff, matter-of-a-fact tone of voice. "But really, what would be the point of it?"

***

Talbor Karonn's quarters were small and rather nondescript. A bed, two low-backed chairs, a desk, and a framed photograph of a severe-looking, much-decorated person that I assumed to be a ruler of some sort were the only furnishings in the little room.

"Korat Delon," Karonn and Tork intoned in unison as they stood reverently erect before the framed portrait. "Leader of the great nation of Karou, we salute you." The two men bowed deeply from the waist to the portrait before turning to their seats which left me to rest my laurels on the Captain's narrow bed.

We had only begun to discuss the means of refueling Star Child when Parlas, the gray-haired young bronze-ring, stuck his head in and requested permission to enter and speak. Karonn nodded to his subordinate, his eyes almost glittering with attentiveness.

"We've checked the stranger's ship and found that it is powered by a type of nuclear material which we do not stock, sir."

"Can his vessel's engine be converted so that it can utilize trasoric fuel?"

"Yes, sir, but such a conversion will take some time."

"Get to it, then. You have my permission."

"Yes, sir. Right away. And – sir...?"

"What else, yeoman?"

"While checking over the craft's instrumentation, we found that it is equipped with radio receiving apparatus. An alien type, of course, but such that is compatible with our own. No transmitter, but I thought.... Well, you know, if the stranger were amenable...."

Silence. Karonn, Parlas, and Tork gazed at me imploringly.

"Yes, of course," I said in a tone that I hoped would imply that I had no choice in the matter. "Use whatever you need of the radio if you think it will help. It's been of no use to me."

"You heard the man, Parlas," Karonn snapped. "Get the radioman out of his bed and get it done."

When Parlas was gone, Karonn and Tork shared a conspiratorial look. "Him?" asked the Captain.

"Those are the rumors," Tork answered.

Seeing my puzzlement, they included me in on the reason for their wonderings: Parlas as the prime suspect as the father of the pregnant crew member's child. Before either man could continue the discussion and air their respective suspicions, a slenderly attractive young woman appeared in the narrow doorway of the room.

"What is it?" asked Karonn.

"The stranger's quarters are ready," she answered sweetly.

"Fine, then. Mister Erin, please follow Miss Dren to your room, if you will. Both Mariss and I have rather pressing duties to attend to. Besides, you must be tired." I got the distinct impression that there was no choice given to me here. I was being summarily dismissed. His tone of voice had become suddenly brusk and businesslike. Perhaps they wanted to be alone with their musings on the identity of the unknown father on board their station. After grasping hands in their culture's manner with each of them, I followed the lovely Miss Dren to my tiny yet adequate quarters. Before she left, I broached the subject of the rumors that were apparently rife aboard Shay-Kah 601.

"I've heard what's been said," she told me warily. "Just a lot of useless, shipboard gossip. Something to help pass the time, that's all."

"But surely you have an opinion as to who the father is," I said. "Do you think it's Parlas?"

She gave me a strange look and then laughed. "I know for a fact that it is not," she said emphatically. And, with a pat to her abdomen to prove the reason for her certain knowledge, she left me with a number of unsaid apologies riding the tip of my tongue.

***

Stars radiate brightly in all corners of my being before the axe falls heavily and the course is set. Then the stars are no more than just light winking through the keyhole of a door in the dark that I know that I shall never reach. Dreams are broken easily by a tender hand shaking my shoulder until my eyes slowly open.

"Wake up, Mister Erin," breathed Miss Dren excitedly. "Wake up. The radio is working again, and they've established contact with home. Your radio parts were all that were needed. Do you understand? Wake up!"

"I'm awake," I grumbled wearily. "Where's the radio shack in this place? I want to hear this for myself."

As Miss Dren walked with me down the hall to the radio room, I chanced a surreptitious glance at the profile of her slender body. Her tummy was as flat as a board, not showing yet. Probably only a month or two gone. We entered the radio room only in time to hear coming from a wall speaker, "End of transmission. And good luck to all of you, wherever you are."

Karonn's face was somber. His solemnity seemed to affect the mood of the entire room, where all nine members of his crew wore the same expression of shocked disbelief. "It's war, Mister Erin," the Captain said. "Involving all three nations on our planet. It's only a matter of time before they destroy themselves. Shiv, the capital city of Karou, has already been hit, if the report that we've just heard is reliable, by two fifty gauge trasoric warheads. Even a near miss by one of those would be sufficient to level the city and a circumference of miles beyond it."

"The transmission we've been hearing is an automatic one," said Grelek, the radioman. "It just keeps repeating the same message, over and over. If it's sending from an orbiting satellite, it could continue until its batteries wear down or it's hit by an enemy missile or laser blast. It's possible that the war had been over for quite a while, and we're only hearing about it now."

"Thanks to Mister Erin," said the Captain, all emotion wrung from his voice so that his words were only sounds produced by rote. There was no longer any humanity to the man.

The signal came through again as Grelek had predicted, the voice of the narrator or copyreader evenly measured as he recounted the situation as it stood at the moment of his expository reading. In the middle of the report, however, the transmission halted, filling the airwaves with a raucous static and then just a hissing silence. The Captain's dark complexion turned sallow, and Seta, the tin ring aspirant I had seen defeated in the Jakor competition, gasped and covered her mouth in shock. Miss Dren, seeming to have come to a sudden realization of what the silence from the speaker meant, started up a terrible din of choking cries.

"Mister Parlas, would you please usher the young lady to her quarters until she can properly compose herself," Karonn ordered sullenly. When the two were finally out of the room, he directed his attention to me.

"Your ship is refueled, Mister Erin, and ready for departure. All anti-gravity apparatus have been removed so that you may land wherever and whenever you so desire. The ship has been equipped with a manual piloting system so that you will have full control of your craft. As soon as your radio equipment has been reinstalled, you may leave whenever you wish."

"Might it not be better if I stayed here?" I asked. "Maybe I could be of some kind of service."

"No, Mister Erin, it would not be better!" Karonn's voice was tense and sharp, like that of an angry, barking dog. Sweat was breaking on his brow. His face was contorted into an angry, frightened grimace.

"We have many things that need the immediate attention of the entire crew," Tork said, pouting like a bereaved parent. And it was only then that I stopped to consider that was just what he was. "You would only be in the way."

"I suppose that I should be leaving right away, then," I said and walked out of the radio shack and headed for my quarters to prepare for my departure. The pitiful sobs and wails of Miss Dren could be clearly heard echoing like the howls of a coyote on the open range throughout the halls of Shay-Kah 601.

***

Starshine, starshine, chants my mind. When shall I ever see dark clouds, wet grass, and rain again? The viewport mists up with my breath as I once more slowly pass the stenciled alien characters that I now recognize as Shay-Kah, followed with a thick dot by the squarely formed numerals 601. My newly installed trasoric reactors click and catch, hum to their optimum setting and I am gone, shooting out of the docking tunnel and out into the black reaches of space. The powerful engines quickly broaden the distance between myself and Karonn and his crew of nine homesick Jakorizas, who shall now never see their homeworld again. I don't care, though, for Star Child now handles even better and more easily than it did before when I had not dominion over its course. I think happily now of new horizons, new suns, and my newly replenished store of food, air, and fuel. Ten minutes do not pass, however, before I look back in the direction of the floating harbor in space that, had circumstances been different, might have been my new home.

Then I am momentarily blinded by the silent, flashing explosion of many tons of nuclear and trasoric materials that instantly blasts Fueling Station Shay-Kah 601 into radioactive space debris and oblivion.

Tears might have welled up in my eyes and choked out my reason had not a winking of beckoning stars caught my attention through the viewport, willing me toward another destiny and, maybe, something I might consider to be a better life. I punch at the colored buttons on the computer console, newly programmed to manual control, and I set a course for what readings have told me was the nearest planet-circled star. With fingers crossed and a vagrant pray in mind, I perform a series of control changes that thrust Star Child into hyper-light-speed drive.

As has been the reason for all prayers throughout mankind's history, I simply hope for the best.

A FALLING JOURNEY
BY ALEX MANN

"Will you remember me?" she asked, gazing at me with sapphire blue eyes clouded by inky blackness. Dressed in dark leather armor, she was every bit the warrior chieftess I had married so long ago. Despite the hardships we had faced on our journey, she hadn't lost that beauty that had struck me stupid as a young man. A sweet zing of smell hit my nostrils, making me look around. The sky rolled with angry dark clouds, threatening to rain.

A single stinging tear fell from my left eye, landing on her forehead to rest like a jewel.

"How could I ever forget you, my gilded unicorn?" My throat was tight as if an orc had seized me by the neck. Cold rushed through my body in waves, and my heart pounded like a blacksmith's hammer. Despite that, I could feel my face was flushed and hot.

She smiled with considerable effort, her once crimson lips now a shade of purple curved into a weak smile. When she reached up to brush my beard, the blonde stubble made a rasping sound as she did. A breath caught in her chest as her body convulsed. The black tendrils in her eyes pulsed and grew. She let out a piercing scream as pain racked through her convulsing body.

I placed a hand on her chest, releasing a bit of my magic to help ease her pain. Pale yellow energy covered my hand as I placed it on her chest, holding her down as the seizure controlled her movements. My magic could do nothing but ease her pain, as little help that was.

She looked up at me, inky black tendrils creeping across her eyes.

Her voice cracked. "My love," she seemed to look not at me but to a point beyond me, "I can see the silver plains. Will you meet me there?"

"Of course, Katrina, It will be like the night of our union, now hush. Save your strength." I sat with her head in my lap, stroking her golden tresses, now dulled by dirt and sweat. She smiled at me, her breathing becoming more labored.

As a new wave of pain ripped through her, she breathed in more than I thought possible. It was as if she couldn't release her held breath. I watched in horror as her eyes went wide in panic for breath. Then her body relaxed, going as limp as a sack of potatoes.

"No! No, no, no." My voice was high and reedy, the grief seizing my heart, stealing my courage. I gathered what energies I could, trying anything to wake Katrina, to get one more second with her. Arcane weaves flowed around us as I tried to do something, anything. It was useless. She was gone.

Feeling a tap on my shoulder, I spun my grief-stricken face to the intruder. I drew a measure of Elicitation weave from around me, forming a plum-sized ball of crackling red energy. Through the watery scope of my vision, I saw my closest friend and ally, Davrik. I let my hold on the magic drop; it fizzled out with a small pop.

He stood a few feet away, scanning the trees before returning his golden-eyed gaze to me and the body I held. His eyes held a cold fury tinged with a softness of grief. Dropping to a knee, he pushed his dark green headband up his forehead, holding back a tide of unruly curly brown shoulder-length hair. The headband was likely a token from one of his recent courtesans.

His blue steel chainmail vest and leather armor creaked as he kneeled. His armor showed many years worth of patches from countless battles, as did the short swords riding at his left hip and above his right shoulder.

Placing a hand on mine, he spoke, "Albert, we have to go. The army of the eye is almost upon us." His voice was higher than you would expect from a man his size. More than once during our travels together, he had stolen the show from an underperforming bard during a performance. "I can hear the outriders a few hundred yards away. We have to go," his final words were muffled by a crack of thunder overhead.

I nodded in agreement, my heart feeling like cold lead in my chest. "Give me a moment, brother." The words caught in my throat. "I won't let her become one of them."

He nodded, walking a few yards away to scout the road behind us. I gently got to my feet, using Katrina's cloak to cushion her head. I removed her delicate platinum ring, placing it on my pinkie. Setting about the grim task of gathering her possessions that could help us, I packed away the few items I could find.

I took her hands in mine and kissed her now cold fingertips, the rain washing my tears away. After folding her hands across her chest, I kissed her forehead one final time. "I love you, my unicorn. I will find you again even if it takes a thousand lifetimes."

I stood from my kneeling position next to her body. Opening my wizard's sight, I found a thick flow of Elicitation magic. Keeping the image of a white-hot flame in my mind, I reached into the flow dragging energy into my hand. As the energy gathered, I could feel the power flowing through my hand like warm oil.

Turning the flame in my mind to a glowing ball of white light, I could feel the flow of magic squirm in my hands like a captured eel. Finally, it solidified into a small hard ball of arcane energy. Holding my ball of energy, I drew a rune above Katrina's body. The lines of magic glowing above her still form. As I completed the ritual, I crushed the ball of energy, speaking, "Flammae."

The rune cracked above her body, engulfing her in pale blue flame, reducing her to a pile of ash to be washed away by the rain. I felt hollow inside a shell of a man. I had nothing left to give as I stoically watched the arcane fire consume Katrina's mortal body. I said a quick prayer over her, "As ashes, we begin, ashes do we return. In the name of the light, guide this soul to the next world."

BOOM! BOOM! BOOM! It sounded as if thunder was rolling overhead, but Davrik and I both knew better. The Army of the Eye was close. With me consumed by grief, we had lost the lead we had gained at Coladaan.

I felt Davrik's strong hand grip my shoulder in reassurance. Not willing to meet his gaze, I stared past him along the road. Suddenly I heard a clap as my cheek stung from Davrik's slap. I stood staring at him in disbelief, the reality of the situation finally coming back into focus.

He spoke with an air of authority that I wasn't used to hearing, The tone he took with his children when they fell out of line. "Steel your heart, Albert. If we are to survive, you need to fight, not just the foes out there," He pointed towards the road, "but the ones that live here too." He put his index finger on my forehead before letting it drop.

Taking a deep breath, I exhaled. Once I got myself under control again, I nodded, "you're right old friend, let's go." I adjusted my pack, tightening the straps. The ground shook under our feet as we looked at each other.

We sped down the road without another word spoken, trying to cover as much distance as possible. Passing by the remains of wagons left by the fleeing refugees, we had to ignore the cries of help from those unwilling to leave their possessions to the approaching army. There was nothing we could do. If we stopped, we would share their unfortunate fate.

The rain had turned the cobblestones into a treacherous path of mud and animal waste, threatening to take us from our feet as we ran on. Davrik outpaced me by a few yards, his long legs carrying him further with each stride. I pushed myself harder to catch up to him; a stitch in my side felt like a dagger between my ribs. I gulped air like a fish out of water, each breath feeling like acid in my lungs. Still, I ran on, adrenaline pushing me forward.

Ahead on the road, Davrik skidded to a stop calling to me between heavy breaths, "Hurry up, I know a shortcut." He bounded off into the trees to the right side of the road. Branches and leaves snapped off as he passed through the brush.

Without breaking my stride, I veered off the road where Davrik had. About ten yards from the path, I encountered a five-foot stream. Leaping across the small creek, I grabbed a low branch to help me reach the other side. My feet hit the muddy bank, water, and muck splashing across my dark green robes.

Trying to stay on my feet, I grabbed onto a thorn bush, the spiked branches biting into my hand. Pulling myself up the bank, I wiped my hand on my robes, leaving a smear of crimson-stained mud. Redoubling my efforts, I followed Davrik along the game trail he led us down. Branches slapped at my face, sharp thorns tearing at the exposed skin on my arms and face.

I lost sight of Davrik as he rounded a tree ahead of me, but I kept up my pace nonetheless. Suddenly I burst from the tree line and was stopped as Davrik caught the collar of my leather breastplate. We had reached the cliffs of Dundry, the jewel of the Rapturian Sea. Even with the clouds of war looming, the city was a sight to behold.

The horseshoe-shaped cliff face sheltered the city. The High Lord's court occupied a small hill against the cliff face, and the city filled in the remaining space leading to the sea. Lightning flashed across the sky reflected in the silver tile rooves that gave the settlement its nickname, "The Shining City."

Walking to the edge of the precipice, Davrik looked, judging the distance. He dropped his pack to the ground, retrieving a large coil of dark rope. I watched the tree line in case our enemies followed us. While Davrik secured the rope, tossing the trailing end over the cliff.

I took a moment to check myself over after the flight through the forest. Blood covered my arms from a multitude of scratches. Retrieving a waterskin from my pack, I rinsed my arms off as best as I could. I took a sip of water to clear my mouth before returning the waterskin. Reaching into a small pouch on my belt, I pulled out a small purple leaf folded into a star shape.

Unfolding the leaf, I used two fingers to smear the oily green substance on my scratches. It released a scent of juniper and cinnamon as it hit my skin. The pain and irritation from the scratches faded, eased by the salve. I joined Davrik at the edge of the cliff, looking down at the buildings below.

From where I stood, it was at least 120 ft. to the roof of the nearest building. The wind made the rope sway back and forth like the flicking of a cat's tail. Turning, I saw Davrik staring into the forest. The tendons in his neck stood out like cable. He had one of his swords in his left hand, knuckles bone white.

Without taking his eyes from the treeline, Davrik spoke in a low tone, "Albert, I think they followed our trail." His voice was like oiled steel. The last time I had heard him like that, we had to fight our way out of Traitor's Well.

As if punctuating his statement, I heard the horn of the army that pursued us. They had indeed found the trail we had taken. I stepped to the tree line gathering a flow of gray Phantasm magic. I wove the magic into a simple illusion, hiding us from anyone still within the treeline.

When I finished the spell, the magic took effect with a shimmer in the air. Satisfied, I turned back to Davrik, "There, that should buy us some time."

Davrik looked my way, and his face lost all color. He reacted on instinct, his arm moving faster than my eye could see. A dagger streaked past my head. I could feel the wind from its passing, inches from my face. Something behind me roared as the dagger impacted with a wet thud. I didn't have to look to know the blade had struck true.

The smell of putrid flesh and sulfur choked my senses as my body sprang into motion. I sprinted from the tree line as fast as my feet would carry me and leaped off the cliff. I barely got my hands on the rope in my flight over the edge. As I fell, I snatched the rope out of the air, the silk weave burning into my hands as I slid down.

The rope ended about twelve feet above the roof. I was traveling too fast to stop myself, and I landed hard on my back. Darkness pulsed at the edges of my vision as I tried to catch my breath. I looked up to see Davrik mere seconds behind me. I rolled out of the way as he landed gracefully on the roof, his heavy boots cracking the silver tiles.

I ignored the pain from my raw, bleeding hands to gather a ball of crackling red magic from the flow around me. Using the energy, I set the rope aflame, hoping that those that followed us wouldn't be willing to risk the drop. Though, I had a suspicion that a fall like that wasn't likely to kill them. A huge black shape watched us from the cliff face.

Continuing our flight, Davrik and I hopped from rooftop to rooftop, finally finding a small shop leading off the roof. Reaching street level, Davrik looked back at the cliff face to see more and more figures joining the first. He fixed me with a grim look. "We have to get to the High Lord. We need to alert him to the danger looming over the city."

"We don't have time." I started towards the harbor, pushing my way through the crowds of people. "We have to get back to the ship, or we're going to be stranded here."

"What do you mean?" He challenged me as we jogged toward our escape. Davrik's voice rose in volume. "We have to give them a chance at least. There are hundreds of thousands of people in this city!"

Stepping into an alley next to a bakery, I pulled Davrik along with me by his collar. I gave him a cold look that left no room for discussion.

"First off, Davrik." A few passersby looked our way before moving on with the growing crowd of people pushing them along. "The messenger we sent ahead has already informed the High Lord of what is coming."

I pointed to the throng of people passing us by. "Do you not see that these people are a hair's breadth away from full-blown panic. They are fleeing, just like we're trying to." I dropped the volume of my voice, ensuring only Davrik could hear me.

"Secondly, You and I know this city is lost. You saw them on the cliff just like I did. We saw the same at Coladaan." I moved to exit the alleyway.

He nodded, his voice low to match my own. "I just wish it wasn't going to be like this again."

Hearing this, I spun around, taking his face in my hands. I could see that despite his iron-clad exterior, his heart was breaking for these people. Using a tone I had heard from him many times before, I said, "We are almost home, old friend. The sooner we get this book back to Salentar, the sooner all this is resolved." I released him and exited the alley into the river of people.

We had to muscle our way through the crowds of people in the merchant quarters. Slimy shysters hawked their wares on every corner, using fear of the coming invasion to boost their sales before fleeing like rats on a sinking ship. I watched as a rotund man wearing a cream-colored linen robe fought with a woman over a wool blanket. I couldn't hear the words exchanged, but his face grew red as they continued to fight over the cloth.

Looking over the crowd, I could see it was a powder keg ready to explode; all it needed was the spark. That came within seconds of me spotting the fight between the disheveled woman and the merchant. The next few seconds seemed to move in slow motion.

The merchant had enough, and he threw a right cross at the

woman. His ham-sized fist connected squarely with her nose, The blow sounding like a cracking melon. The woman fell back, acting as a barrier between the merchant and the crowd. She hit the ground, and her dress fluttered a bit before falling to rest in the mud. A few of the members of the crowd looked at the woman before looking at the merchant.

The entire crowd in the area stopped everything. It grew silent, and then chaos erupted. The crowd flew into a mob rage, those closest to the merchant attacking him for what he did while others jumped into the fray defending the merchant. As Davrik and I rushed through the crowd, we ended up in a dead-end alleyway.

Looking back towards the crowd, I saw a few bloody men traversing the alley, their blood lust not yet slaked. Davrik found a door as he moved further down the alley away from the main street. He booted it open, the inner lock and crossbar shattering under his assault. We ducked inside, replacing the door as well as we could before struggling to block the door with a heavy table.

We made our way through the empty building. It was oppressively hot in the building. Along the back wall, I saw many small open forges. Curiosity got the better of me, and I stepped closer to check the contents. Each one contained a pot of molten glass, kept hot by a set of runes along the rim of each forge. We stepped out of the hot workshop and found the storeroom and the door outside.

I picked up a star-shaped glass bottle, tucking it into a pouch on my belt. A portion of this master's craft would survive the razing of the city tucked into my belt pouch. Cracking the outer door a few inches, he checked the street. He waved me forward, and we slipped out of the shop.

We continued our journey towards the harbor with relative ease, with the violence contained behind us. We braved the crowd pushing people out of our way as we made our way to the ship that would carry us away from here. As we made our way past dock forty-three, a sound made the entire city collectively freeze.

The tolling of a great brass bell echoed across the city. The citizens all held their breath as the bell sounded. I felt someone pulling on my arm. Looking over, I saw Davrik pulling on my arm. That spurred me into motion, and we ran through the crowd. Cries from those we knocked over faded with the rising tide of fear quickly rippling through the crowd.

After a few paces, all hell broke loose as explosions tore through the city, sending the citizens into an animalistic fury. I watched as people abandoned their possessions and fought to escape any way they could. Davrik and I were caught in the midst of it and had to fight our way out. I pushed young and old out of my way, receiving my share of hits for it.

Making our push to the dock we needed, A large man confronted me, smelling of sour ale and old bratwurst. Various unknowable stains covered his tattered clothes. He held a wickedly sharp Jambiya in a dirty fist. His eyes flared a glowing pale blue, and he rushed towards me.

I leaned away from his first strike. The horizontally slash

whistled past my face. If I had been a heartbeat slower, he would've opened my throat with that slash. He was aggressive, attacking in rapid succession. I dodged his attacks until one found its mark, cutting a long slash across my arm.

His next attack was his last. As he thrust the blade at my face, I caught his wrist and, in one smooth motion, disarmed him and broke his ankle with a well-placed stomp. I slipped his knife into my belt, leaving him on the ground to howl in pain. I had lost sight of Davrik but quickly found him a few yards away, looking through the crowd for me.

Reunited, we finally reached dock sixty-seven; it was just as crowded as any other part of the harbor. But the gangway leading to our ship was clear of any panicked citizens. Although, they gathered at the bottom of the ramp in hopes they could get a spot.

The ship was a work of art; constructed of marble oak by Raznothi artisans from the far north. Crimson-dyed sails mirrored the leaves of the marble oak. Being slim and shallow of the draft, the ship could easily handle most major rivers and the crossing to Freeman's Port.

We approached the ship, and I could see a great bear of a man standing at the top of the ramp. His sun-tanned chest was bare under a mottled red leather vest. A thick oak club hung from a leather cord around his wrist, his loose brown linen pants billowing in the wind. He shifted in place on his bare feet, watching for trespassers.

I watched as one brave fool, with more balls than brains, tried his luck with the man guarding the ship. He stepped forward, pulling a knife from his belt. "You can't keep us off the ship. It's your duty to help us escape!" he cried, charging forward. The guard brought his club down with one fluid motion upon the fool's head, crumpling him. He kicked the body into the bay, waiting for the next person to test him.

He addressed the gathered crowd, his voice booming above their heads. "This is my ship, The Wind Strider, and neither she nor I are beholden to anyone. The only way you're getting on there is with my passage medallion, or you'll end up like that idiot." Pointing to the body in the water next to the ship.

Davrik and I pushed our way to the gangway. The man readied himself for us to rush him as the last man had. I reached into one of my belt pouches, producing a bronze amulet in the shape of a heron in flight. It had been given to me when Davrik and I had departed from the ship. I held it high above my head, yelling to the man, "Captain Jerund, permission to come aboard?"

He waved us closer, taking the medallion from me. He studied it for a second before saying, "come aboard! And be quick about it." I hurried onto the ship with Davrik a half step behind me. Hearing the cries from the crowd, I had to block it out and focus on my mission.

I heard a splash as the captain kicked the gangway into the bay, taking the two men that had tried to rush the ship with it. Captain Jerund cut the ropes securing the ship to the harbor, each making a snapping sound from the tension. He yelled at the crew, "to 'yer places herrene, we have somewhere to be."

At the captain's command, the sailors all rushed below decks, running out the long, wide, paddled oars. I stumbled a bit as the ship lurched into motion. I breathed a sigh of relief as we began to turn to the open ocean. Taking the star-shaped glass bottle from my pouch, I admired its beauty, for a moment, before returning it to my bag.

The sickly smell of burning homes and seared flesh was already drifting from the city. I looked back to the harbor as we fled to the safety of the open ocean. Flames consumed the harbor, up to dock thirty-eight. The shop that I had picked up the bottle from was no more. The only reminder is the star-shaped bottle in my belt pouch.

The boat slid away from the docks leaving those multitudes of people to whatever cruel fate was in store for them. I watched as the Army of the Eye finally reached the docks. Hundreds of orcs, men, and elves bearing the black armor of the eye swept through the harbor, cutting down all that stood in their path. Turning my wizard's sight to the sun, I raised both hands, pulling as much Divine and Elicitation as I could. I felt the power flow into me like warm honey.

I revealed with the power I was gathering. Although I knew that the draw of magic would destroy me, I continued to draw as much arcane weave as I could. I felt an immense pressure behind my eyes, and my body thrummed with the magic I now held. I turned my gaze to the docks and raised my right hand.

In a low voice, I spoke a short phrase, "Di urunt has feras in cinere." Finishing the incantation, I turned my hand palm out towards the docks and the army that ravaged them. Suddenly a bar of crackling yellow light shot from my hand, and I swept it across the piers. Although it only lasted a few seconds, it had the desired effect.

Those struck by the bar howled in agony as the heat from the magic boiled their organs. The spell winked out, and I swooned but stayed on my feet. I had bought those remaining on the docks a few minutes at most. I hoped that would be enough to help them escape.

As the ship approached the sea gates to the harbor, guards on the walls were frantically trying to work the levers. The massive stone doors began to open, letting the first few ships out that had reached it before us.

Despite my best efforts, the flood of Eye soldiers pressed forward to the controls for the gate. As I drew another cord of Elicitation magic from the flow around me, I spotted something that made me drop the magic I'd drawn. Katrina stood at the end of the closet dock.

A white gossamer dress clung to the feminine curves of her warrior's body; it moved as if touched by a gentle breeze. Her golden tresses swayed in time with her dress. She held out a hand to me in farewell, mouthing something to me. I ran to the quarter-deck, straining past the railing to see what she was mouthing to me.

A smile crept across my face as I watched her mouth the words, 'I Love You.' My mind wandered to thoughts of that night in the hills above Ninhen Rest. We had stopped there on our way to Draken Haus to pick up a few rare items from Hermus Nuthro. His return from across the Dragon Spine mountains had been profitable, and he had a deal with my father.

We had decided to stay in the hills instead of the inn. The clientele looked less than reputable, and it was a nice night for a campout. After setting up our camp, we lay next to the small fire, listening to the soft pops as the pitch boiled away to steam cracking the wood. My fingertips traced small circles over her back as we lay together.

She shuddered under my touch, gooseflesh spreading from where my fingers touched her skin. I continued rubbing her back, moving lower until I cupped her buttocks. Giggling slightly, she swung a leg over to straddle me as we lay next to the little cracking fire. I reached up, stroking her face, counting the freckles on her face. As Katrina smiled, she moved my hand from her face to her neck and beyond.

A sledgehammer blow to my chest brought me out of my memories; A single tear dripped from my eye. I looked down to see a black arrow shaft protruding from my chest just below the sternum. My breath wouldn't come; it felt like an ox was sitting on my chest. Falling to the deck, I gasped for breath as I heard boots rushing toward me.

I looked up to see Davrik drop to his knees beside me. He

placed a gentle hand on my chest, trying to hold me still. The wound felt as if someone had poured acid into it, burning the flesh and poisoning my blood. He grabbed a knife from his belt and began cutting the straps of my leather breastplate, each movement bringing a fresh wave of pain to me.

My head rolled to the side as Davrik finished getting my armor off. The waves bobbed beyond the deck as I stared through the bars of the deck railing. A vision of white gossamer silk filled my sight, and I saw Katrina kneel next to me, taking my hand in hers. Davrik's voice faded away as I stared at her. I closed my eyes with a smile on my face. The darkness took me away, and I felt myself fall.

I fell for endless hours, or were it years, decades perhaps. The eternal darkness was a shroud of comfort better than any in a mother's arms. I had no sense beyond contentment in the vast tenebrosity around me. As I fell, pinpoints of light pulsed around me, bringing memories not my own. I closed my eyes, attempting to block out the light to embrace the darkness and its comforts. Stronger, the lights pulsed, pressing their own light and strange images onto my consciousness. No matter which way I turned, the light pressed on until finally, I opened my eyes. Imagines of a surreal world spun around me; the darkness was gone now beyond my reach.

WRITTEN IN THE SAND
By Michael Onofrio

It was a warm day. Not a hot day, where sweat runs down your forehead in rivers and the only refuge from heat stroke is the air conditioning in your car or house, but the type of day where you can wear jeans or shorts and be completely comfortable. The kind of day built just for evenings on the lake. This type of day found Nick and Cameron in Simon's dusty Subaru hatchback, crawling down the highway towards the lake for an evening of drinking beer and talking about the types of things that make sense when you are in your early twenties. As the office parks and strip malls of the city slowly melted away, the question of where exactly the evening was to be spent was raised. "It's beautiful, man," said Simon, "I've only been there a couple times, but there hasn't been a single person around whenever I've been."

"Probably a good thing it was deserted," thought Nick, as he knew that most of Simon's visits had been with girls he had been trying to impress. As Cameron queued up another song, Nick felt his eyelids drooping and eventually slumped onto the back of his seat; completely asleep.

"Hey Nick, we're here." Nick opened his eyes. In front of him was a mass of shrubs and trees that stretched out from side to side as far as he could see. He would not have believed they were at a lake if he couldn't have vaguely heard the sounds of small waves lapping at the shore. Stretching, Nick groggily opened the car door and stepped out. Eager to get down to the lake and start the evening, Cameron and Simon's towels whipped out of sight down a small trail that snaked its way back through the trees. Struggling to wake up, Nick grabbed his towel and the cooler and shut the car door. Slightly tripping over his feet, he started down the trail towards the beach. It was fortunate that someone had wanted to reach this beach. As if there hadn't been a trail, Nick wouldn't have been able to walk through the dense growth. Shrubs and saplings grew densely up to shoulder height on either side of Nick. The dense growth spread out on either side of Nick for what seemed miles, all overshadowed by a thick mix of pines and oaks that let small rays of sunlight pierce the forest floor. After about fifteen minutes of walking, the forest suddenly opened to reveal a beach. About a football field long, the beach was covered in fine white sand that slowly turned darker as it got closer to the water's edge. On the far edge of each side of the beach, huge willow trees hung out over the water closing the area off from view from either side. Looking out over the lake, Nick could not see a single boat cruising the water or house on the far shore. From what he could tell, this lake seemed to be truly off the beaten path and with the exception of the path through the woods, untouched by civilization. Despite the novelty of this privacy, Nick could not help but feel unnerved. He felt a strange kind of lonely fear that he associated with looking at the quiet streets of the suburbs at night or abandoned industrial parks in the city. These places seemed like they should be teeming with life and activity but, for some strange reason, were deserted.

Shattering this feeling, a beer can suddenly landed in front of Nick with a soft thud, throwing sand up into the air. Nick grinned and ran over to join Cameron and Simon, who had just turned on the music and were talking loudly on the water's edge. Conversation continued for hours, with topics ranging from the serious (the strains of one's relationships) to the unimportant (which villain from Dragon Ball Z was strongest). It was the kind of conversation you can only have with friends you've known your whole life. As the sky turned from blue to light pink, Nick suggested they go into the water before it got too dark. Simon and Cameron agreed, and once shirts had been discarded, they made their way out into the water. For about an hour, the boys amused themselves trying to catch small fish and the crawdads that scuttled across the bottom of the lake, shouting each other's names loudly when they spotted something particularly large. The water was clear enough to make out the muddy brown shapes as they dove to the bottom. Surfacing from a particularly intense chase after a small turtle, Nick glanced towards the beach. As he watched, he seemed to notice something large and dark slither back into the water. He lost track of the shape as it moved into the bright patch of sun on the water and then disappeared. Thinking it must have been a large turtle or beaver, Nick shrugged and began making his way to shore. Dragging his feet through the thick sand, Nick made his way over to where he had seen the shape on the beach. As he moved closer, he saw some sort of shapes drawn in the sand. Upon closer inspection, he saw they were words. Scrawled in large shaky letters, two words were written in the sand:

Who first

"Simon, Cameron," called Nick, "come over here and look at this." Nick heard splashes of his friends leaving the water as he stared at the words in the sand. All around the words were splotches of dark green algae connected by strands of slime and mud. Nick bent down and touched the letters, inadvertently covering his hands in the thick phlegmy substance. As he stood up, Cameron walked over.

"Who first," said Cameron, "what does that mean?"

"I have no clue," said Nick, "Somebody else probably wrote it when they were here." In a dark back corner of Nick's mind, he couldn't help but wonder if what had slithered back into the water had written it.

"Simon," called Cameron, not looking back, "what do you think?"

Silence.

"Simon?" called Nick.

Silence, punctuated only by the quiet slapping of the water against the beach.

Finally turning to look behind them, Nick and Cameron saw only Simon's towel lying in the sand.

"Where is he, man?" asked Nick. "You guys were both out there, and I thought he came back with you."

"We both dived under when you called us over," stammered Cameron. "I lost track of him underwater and didn't look when I got out."

"Did he have keys with him?" asked Nick. "We're screwed if he did."

"Let's check his towel. That's the only spot they'd be beside his pocket."

With the franticness of people who know they are one step away from disaster, Nick and Cameron sprinted towards the towels and cooler. Nick grabbed the towel and shook it. Loose chunks of sand fell and reintegrated themselves with the beach. "NO," shouted Cameron and began frantically scooping sand with his hands, desperately trying to unearth keys that were in the pocket of their missing friend. With a loud crack, Cameron swore, having ripped a fingernail off on a piece of wood buried in the sand.

"We'll be fine," said Nick shakily, "I didn't take my phone when we went swimming."

"I'll call my parents and the police, and we'll figure out what happened and get out of here."

With fumbling fingers, Nick pulled out his phone and turned it on. Greeting him were the dreaded words: no service. Nick swore loudly and plopped to the ground. "Dude, don't worry," said Cameron, "I sent a text before we walked down here, so I know there's service where we parked the car." "We just have to walk back to the car." Reinvigorated with a shred of hope, Nick slowly stood up and started following Cameron back up the beach. As they walked up the slope towards the tree line, the pink sunset became closer to dark blue as the light began to fade. As twilight progressed, Nick and Cameron walked along the line of trees, searching in vain for the path that had led them to this isolated patch of what had seemed to be paradise hours ago. Abandoning any ideas of a clean escape, Nick and Cameron seized up their courage and pushed through the shrubs into the forest, deciding to forget their search for the path.

The forest that had seemed beautiful in the evening was now dark and ominous. Gone were the chirps of birds and chittering of squirrels. The forest was silent except for the cracking of sticks and leaves as the boys pushed their way through. Small vines tripped their feet and thorns tore at their skin. With each grueling step forward, Nick felt as though the vines and shrubs were purposefully impeding his progress as each step got more and more difficult.

"Hold up, Nick."

"What is it?"

"Just hold up," said Cameron.

He seemed to be straining to hear. Despite them not moving, something was crashing through the bushes behind them. Nick and Cameron, frozen with fear, as they could hear heavy breathing and the drip of some form of liquid hitting the leaves of the shrubs beneath. Darkness has descended on the forest almost completely, almost completely obscuring their vision. Suddenly, the sounds coming from behind them stopped. Trying to discern anything in the oppressive darkness of the forest, Nick and Cameron squinted at where the sound had been coming from.

Tearing through the quiet night air, the scream of someone who could only be in horrific pain came from behind the beach.

"Is that Simon?" stammered Cameron.

"No clue," said Nick shakily, "but we have to find out. We can't leave him if he's in trouble."

With trembling feet, Nick and Cameron turned around and began to make their way out of the forest. Nick noticed it was a lot easier going back the way they came than it was to go forward, almost as if the forest wanted them to return to the beach. Stumbling out of the growth, it became a little easier to see, as the thick forest canopy had filtered out much of the remaining sunlight. As they ran across the beach, trying to locate the source of the scream, Nick saw something make a large splash in the calm water about 20 yards off the beach. As the ripples began to fade, a pair of swim trunks slowly floated to the surface in a pool of blood and muck. Cameron gasped and began running into the water.

"What the hell are you doing," shouted Nick. "Whatever did that is probably right there."

"I don't care," yelled Cameron. "His keys might still be in the pockets."

Nick swore but didn't argue, as he wanted to leave this place as much as Cameron did. He stood still, watching Cameron swim slowly out towards the swim trunks. A small spider crawled across Nick's foot, causing him to look down. Scrawled across the sand in the same shaky lettering as before were the words:

Who next

"Cameron," yelled Nick. "Get out of the water."

With a sudden splash, Cameron was yanked under the surface of the water, mere feet away from the swimsuit. The water frothed and spurted as Cameron seemed to desperately fight with what was pulling him under. Suddenly, the water turned scarlet red. With a great splash, Cameron suddenly broke the surface of the water. What was visible was not a pretty sight. Half of Cameron's face had been ripped off, with an eyeball dangling from its socket. His teeth were a jumbled white and red mess where his mouth had been, and the nose was pulpy cartilage. With a disturbing, gurgling scream, Cameron was yanked back beneath the water. The pool of red grew. Nick stood motionless at the beach. The sudden weight of his isolation crashed down upon him. It was just him and whatever had taken the lives of his two best friends. His knees suddenly losing strength, Nick collapsed to his knees at the water's edge. Any strength or desire to leave was gone, as he had a feeling that what had killed his friends would not let him leave. He stared at the ground, waiting to be taken. As he stared, something strange began to happen in the sand. It was as if a small brown stick was standing up without prompting and writing in the sand by itself. As Nick watched, the stick slowly wrote the words:

Who's last?

Despite knowing his fate was sealed, Nick refused to say his own name. He sat staring at the words for what seemed like hours.

The stick that had written the words suddenly began to rise out of the sand. It grew longer and longer until a hand burst from the sand, the stick having actually been a finger with long dirty nails. The hand slammed into the sand and pushed down. Nick felt his bladder and bowels empty as the creature rose out of the sand. It was horrible beyond comprehension. Most likely due to its time in the lake, it was the same putrid green and brown color as the algae that coated its body. Its mouth seemed to stretch three-quarters of the way around its head and was filled with rows of teeth, some so jammed together they crossed over each other. On its head were lidless orange eyes that contained more intelligence than one would want from a lake creature. Dangling from its chest were a collection of tentacles that seemed to move with free will, snaking through the air. The arms were long and spindly and ended in hands with 6-inch claws, sharp as knives. All Nick could do was stare at the creature that had claimed his friends' lives. The putrid smell of sulfur and algae combined became too much, and Nick vomited at the creatures. The creature laughed in Cameron's voice, a perfect imitation. It began to speak to Nick in Simon's tone, but Nick was too terrified to care what it said, too numb with fear to register the reason it had for killing time. He was so desensitized that he didn't see the tentacles' ends open into shark-like mouths. He didn't even feel it when one shot into his chest, and the other ripped his face from his skull.

HUNTED

By E. L. McKenzie

Kill. Times ten. Or be killed. Great!

***

"Gentlemen," Ogre began. "Most of you are veterans of the hunt. However, we have two rookies. They are Hunters 9 and 10."

There was no looking around the room. Ogre spoke behind an opaque, bullet-proof glass. Each of the ten hunters occupied a self-contained cubicle unit. They could all see Ogre's image, but not each other. Anonymity reigned. No one knew anyone else. Ogre's voice was digitally altered.

$10 million entry fee for each hunter. Winner takes all – well, except for the $50 million Ogre kept for sponsoring the hunt. So, winner takes half.

"For those of you returning, welcome back. For you newbies, welcome."

***

It has been 37 days since Prey arrived. His last memory before arriving is a drunken night celebrating with one of his sports-management clients – an up-and-coming baseball player recently promoted to AAA. He recalls getting into the Uber...and then waking up in this strange place.

The experience is both terrifying and weird. He's incarcerated, held in something like a dungeon. Except the prison cell is huge and luxurious. Memory foam bed. Steam shower. Work-out room second to none. Television with a huge database of movies and TV shows for consumption – but, of course, no internet connectivity. Delicious, nutritious meals are served three times daily. Fully stocked refrigerator and pantry. Every comfort one could desire except companionship or freedom.

Ogre provided Prey the rules upon arrival. Prey has spent his time working. In 37 days, he has chiseled and prepared his already lean, fit body with a combination of aerobic exercise, weight lifting, yoga, and meditation. He has scrupulously studied every inch of the detailed tropical island map Ogre provided. He is as ready as possible.

***

Ogre continued, "I have meticulously covered the ground rules with each of you hunters. For those of you returning, none of this is new. But I insist on doing this again with all of you together. Each of you will find the printed rules in your backpack. The Competitor, whose name for game purposes is Prey, has them, too. And remember, The Competitor has been here for six weeks preparing and acclimatizing to allow for the best, most competitive experience possible."

"The rules are simple. The game concludes only when The Competitor is dead – or all of you are. During the game, you are not allowed back into The Compound. No exceptions. If you're having a heart attack, too bad. If The Competitor has injured you, too bad. If you want to quit, too bad. The game continues until it concludes, and you participate until the conclusion of the game. Questions about this?"

Silence.

"In addition, and this is important, key really. You have been provided a gun with two bullets for self-defense. You may only use it if you are attacked, not if you are attacking. A violation of this rule will result in removal from the game, forfeiture of your entry fee, and you won't be allowed to participate in future hunts. Do understand The Competitor does not have a gun, but if he dispatches one of you, he likely will, and he is not constrained by this rule."

***

Suddenly, Ogre enters The Competitor's room, and he's dressed like the Phantom of the Opera. If not for the circumstances, he'd look hilarious.

"Mr. Prey, do you have any questions before the festivities begin?"

"Seriously?" Prey asks as he considers killing him. The mammoths on either side of Ogre would probably keep that from happening.

"I have read the rules repeatedly," he continues. "Why? Why are you doing this?" He's sweating and visibly upset.

Ogre remains impassive. "Mr. Prey, this is your opportunity to clarify any lingering questions you have about the game. I recommend you focus. Is there anything I can address for you before we begin?"

He can't bring himself to ask the obvious questions. If he kills everyone, does he really get to walk away? And with $10 million for killing ten people?

"Why did you pick me?"

"You're a great athlete," Ogre explained. "You lettered in four sports in high school, two in college, and would have been a great NBA point guard if you were a little taller. You have stayed fit and sharp. I wanted someone who would provide a challenge for my clients."

"Okay, and are your clients all athletes, too?"

He chuckles. "Hardly. They're all idiots, but they're useful. To provide you or any other competitor at least a fighting chance, I require that all my clients be past 50. I don't bring in any competitors over 30. At 25, and especially given the last six weeks to train, you have an advantage over these guys. Of course, there are more of them, and they have weapons. But, you know, they're paying, so...."

***

"Let me tell you a little bit about The Competitor." Ogre briefly introduces Prey's physical prowess. "So, he's younger than you, he's more athletic than you, and he's fighting for his life. Don't underestimate his abilities. He may not be an outdoorsman, but I assure you he's properly motivated. And remember, he has night vision goggles, and you don't. So, he can find you. Be careful at night."

"Any further questions?" Silence.

"Okay, we start bright and early. The Competitor will be released tonight. We'll draw for starting times in the morning at the gate. You'll head out in fifteen-minute increments beginning at 6 a.m."

***

And with that, Prey's outside. It's pitch black. He knows the hunters won't start until morning, so he has some time to prepare. He moves a little way down the wall, sits, rummages through his backpack, and takes out his night vision goggles.

He has prepared for this his whole life. Not being hunted like some wild animal but competing for "survival." Sure, it's usually to win a football game or some other meaningless contest. But it's still competition. These are the longest odds he has faced, but the prize is much more consequential, too. He gets to live. The $10 million is irrelevant.

***

"Hunter 3, you are released," Ogre declares after drawing the first name. And with that, at 6 a.m. sharp and the break of morning, the first hunter rushes through the gate. For the next two-plus hours, another hunter deploys every 15 minutes. Soon the Park, Ogre's own private, secluded island, is scattered with hunters seeking Prey.

***

Prey has always been a very good athlete, maybe even close to great. There were always guys bigger, stronger, faster, and all-around better at any sport he played. But he beat them routinely. Why? Because he prepared better. He thought more. He outsmarted them. That's it. And he intuits that to survive this contest, he will have to play his greatest game ever.

Strategy. He moved swiftly to the other side of the island, giving himself more than two miles of cushion before the first hunter was released. He dug his three-part hole – one-part living/sleeping quarters, barely big enough for him to stretch out, one-part latrine, and one-part trap. Given the quarter's structure was well off the trail, Prey knew it was unlikely he would snag a predator. But he was ready. In the meantime, he settled into the dug-out fortress to sleep, conserve energy, and wait for the hunters to become frustrated and careless.

***

Hunter 9 rushes out of The Compound, intent on finding Prey first. He's fourth out of The Compound, and it's only 6:45 on Day 1. Confidant. Fit. Brutal. He knows he can handily defeat Prey if he can just find him first. Then add $50 million to his already bulging net worth.

***

4:35 p.m. Day 1, and Prey already hears someone stalking through the underbrush. He quietly pushes up the limb allowing a view, and peers toward the noise. Sure enough, Hunter 9 is less than 100 feet away, looking down, creeping through the growth.

All the hunters' outfits are numbered, and Prey suspects Hunter 9 is a rookie. It's early in the game, and he hopes the hunter is full of adrenaline and careless. He worked hard to hide all signs of digging the hole and camouflaging it, but he had scant time to ensure all evidence was hidden. He picked up the chosen rock, took his position, and waited.

***

Crash! Prey is still looking at Hunter 9 when someone crashes through the false forest floor into his trap. Shit. Prey's on him instantly, ending Hunter 3's life in moments, the spraying blood irrelevant to his urgent mission.

As soon as he finds Hunter 3's gun, he looks up to see Hunter 9 standing over him, struggling to draw an arrow. He sees Prey and the gun too late as the bullets pierce his chest.

***

Prey is in a sprint. He knows the noise will draw the other hunters. He took one moment to grab his backpack and Hunter 9's. He planned for this. He mapped his exit. All his supplies were already in his backpack, ready to go. He would not die simply because he could not think through scenarios.

***

Hunter 2 arrived at the death scene first. He knew others would be behind him shortly, so he scavenged all he could from his two dead competitors before anyone else arrived. Hunter 1 startled him just as he finished his reconnaissance of the site.

They lowered their guns when they saw the yellow of the other.

"You already steal all their stuff?" Hunter 1 asked casually.

"You'd be disappointed in less, right?" Hunter 2 responded. As he spoke, he gestured to the scene. "I know you've done this more times than me, but I've been out here a fair number of times. I've never seen anything like this."

"No, getting two guys at once is a new one for me, too. But, hell, you have to give the guy credit. He really is fighting for his life."

As he finished, the Clean-Up Crew arrived. Per the rules of the game, hunters were required to move out of sight immediately. Hunters 1 and 2 turned and departed in different directions.

***

Five hundred yards from his encampment, Prey slowed to a walk. He carefully picked his way another two hundred yards uphill and well off the trail to a secluded spot. He knew this island from studying the map for six weeks. He sat. And watched.

Hunter 1 was just arriving as Prey focused his binoculars. The two hunters spoke briefly before a camouflage-colored Humvee arrived and ejected six burly men in white hazmat suits. From tirelessly reading the rules and "what to expect" tutorial from Ogre, he assumed this must be the Clean-Up Crew.

As they arrived, the hunters departed in different directions, and thankfully not towards him.

***

Moments later, Hunter 10 arrived on the scene, surveyed the damage, and approached the Clean-Up Crew Team Leader. "I need to speak to Ogre."

"Sir, you aren't supposed to be here. Per the rules, once the Clean-Up Crew arrives on-site, hunters are required to leave the area immediately."

"Now!" Hunter 10 demanded. "This is bullshit. I didn't sign up for this. We are the hunters, not the other way around."

The noise was loud enough that Prey could make out what Hunter 10 was saying. The Team Leader spoke more quietly.

"Sir, if you don't vacate this scene immediately, I'll have to call security. I have no choice."

Hunter 10 blanched, turned, and strode off.

***

Prey had his next target. And he knew what to do. Slowly, methodically, quietly, Prey dug a trench for his equipment with just enough extra space to sleep. At 6:00 p.m. on Day 1, Prey was already a successful hunter. He began creeping his way back to The Compound.

***

Hunter 10 arrived moments after Prey took his pre-planned position to surreptitiously watch the activity at The Compound. Prior to heading to the other side of the island the night before, he had prepared this spot. It wasn't the logical spot, nor the best for spying, and that was the point. The hunters would look for him in more logical positions.

Hunter 10 began banging on the large compound doors. "Open up. Now. I demand to see Ogre."

Silence.

***

Prey counted on Hunter 10's carelessness. It paid off. Hunter 10 paced around the fortress and screamed for well over an hour. Dusk fell. Prey prepared. Hunter 10 was not two hundred yards from The Compound on a well-traveled trail when Prey crept up behind him and plunged his knife deep into the hunter's neck. As he did so, he wrapped his left arm around Hunter 10's face, fully covering his mouth and stifling the weak scream that emanated.

As he drug the lifeless body off the trail, Prey stopped and listened. Silence. Good. He quickly scavenged food, bullets, a tent, a sleeping bag, an air mattress, and re-supply directions. He then retreated a safe distance to watch. More silence. No Clean-Up

Crew.

Prey decided to sit and think rather than return to his makeshift campsite. After an hour, he quietly worked his way back down to Hunter 10. Quickly and methodically, he stripped away the yellow pants, yellow jacket, and headgear, stuffing them into his already overflowing backpack. And just as quickly, he was gone, using night vision goggles to quietly work his way back to camp.

***

Ogre chuckled. "These dimwits think they can run out of here and kill some poor soul simply because they're rich and have a bow and arrow," he mused. And he doesn't know about Hunter 10 yet.

"Sir?" Team Leader interrupted the moment of bemusement. "Hunter 10 has not moved in hours. I suspect Prey tracked him after his blow-up at The Compound."

Ogre pondered this development. "I won't say anything in The Daily Update. You and the crew can go look in the morning."

"Yessir." And with that Team Leader departed.

***

Hunter 1 was the only recipient of the first issue of The Daily Update, Ogre's daily publication of the prior day's events, and anything else he deemed newsworthy. It was handed out from 9:00

to 10:00 each morning at The Compound doors to any hunter arriving during that time:

The Daily Update – Day 2

Prey killed Hunter 3 and Hunter 9 yesterday. In addition, he took their supplies, including their guns.

Standard Footnote: The Daily Update provides daily facts and updates Ogre considers appropriate. It does not opine, speculate, or provide information from prior days.

***

Prey slept hard. He couldn't believe it. He had killed three people only hours earlier. One he coldly stalked and executed. But he nestled into his dugout, ate a protein bar, drank some water, and slept soundly until the sun came up.

***

Hunter 1 was the veteran. This was his ninth hunt, and he had won three times. When he was younger, African safaris interested him. But at this point, he had killed every animal imaginable, legally or illegally, with every weapon imaginable. This was far more interesting.

Prey was smart. This kid was savvier than most. On his first hunt, he saw something like this. But he was cautious. Four hunters died. The fifth would have died, but Hunter 1 heard the commotion, came in and killed the hunted. If Hunter 1 had not been nearby, who knows how many more hunters that competitor would have killed – maybe all of them.

***

Prey rested all of Day 2. He had no intention of venturing out during daylight. By design, he sat at a fairly high point. He spent much of the day peering out, watching the hunters' movements to begin establishing patterns.

***

Hunter 8 completed his fourth lap around the island and through all the trails. A man of discipline and rigor, he had well established his routine for the hunt. He was determined to find The Competitor, to fully engage in the hunt.

***

Prey watched as Hunter 8's pattern emerged. He formulated his Day 3 plan, ate a protein bar, and went to sleep.

***

As Hunter 8 rounded the bend on the northwest end of the island, he saw Hunter 10 running towards him. Per the rules of the game, he turned to retrace his prior position for two hundred yards and then figure out where to go next. "Wait, wait," the figure in Hunter 10's gear yelled. Hunter 8 paused and turned around. Prey quickly closed the distance, ran up to Hunter 8 breathlessly exclaiming, "you have to…" – and while he was speaking, pulled his gun, pushed the barrel within inches of a surprised Hunter 8's eyes, and pulled the trigger.

Wasting little time, Prey quickly confiscated Hunter 8's gun and food and sprinted into the trees.

***

Hunters 6 and 7 both faced similar fates on Day 4. Prey determined there was a certain trust amongst the hunters. He calculated that would endure for the remainder of the day, and then the other hunters would figure out his deception. He further calculated that the hunter numbers on the yellow gear represented level of experience, with Hunter 1 being the most experienced and Hunter 10 the least. He was correct.

Therefore, he exploited the lack of experience on the newer hunters. Before the end of Day 4, he had eliminated six, mostly the least experienced.

***

Hunters 1, 2, 4, and 5 all arrived on the morning of Day 5 for The Daily Update. Only Hunter 1 had the prior updates.

The Daily Update – Day 4

Hunters 6, 7, and 8 all died today. Each was killed on a trail with a single gunshot to the head. Each hunter has only two bullets. Therefore, these three hunters were killed by bullets from multiple hunters' munitions today.

Standard Footnote: The Daily Update provides daily facts and updates Ogre considers appropriate. It does not opine, speculate, or provide information from prior days.

***

Prey was oddly exhilarated from his Day 4 success. At the same time, he knew sometimes after a flurry of success, it was best to sit back and reassess. He retreated to his underground bunker. He spent his nights building a second and third bunker on different parts of the island, stocking each with necessities he had taken from his victims. He otherwise laid low through the remainder of the first week, resting, performing limited resistance exercises, thinking, and planning.

***

The four wary hunters visited The Compound daily to receive updates and resupply as necessary. Given the swift dispatch of hunters during the first four days, expectations were high each morning. However, each day they found The Daily Update underwhelming:

The Daily Update – Day 5

Nothing to report.

Standard Footnote: The Daily Update provides daily facts and updates Ogre considers appropriate. It does not opine, speculate, or provide information from prior days.

The Daily Update – Day 6

Nothing to report.

Standard Footnote: The Daily Update provides daily facts and updates Ogre considers appropriate. It does not opine, speculate, or provide information from prior days.

The Daily Update – Day 7

Nothing to report.

Standard Footnote: The Daily Update provides daily facts and updates Ogre considers appropriate. It does not opine, speculate, or provide information from prior days.

The Daily Update – Day 8

Heavy rain expected for the next several days.

Standard Footnote: The Daily Update provides daily facts and updates Ogre considers appropriate. It does not opine, speculate, or provide information from prior days.

***

Prey counted on the rain. Each bunker was built with heavy precipitation in mind. He had taken enough gear such that each shelter had a roof of tent material to repel and direct water as best as possible considering the higher calling for invisibility. His sleeping area sat higher, so any water that did get in would drain away. And the floor of each sleeping area was a rainfly.

At this point, he knew the preferred campsites of three of the four hunters; he still had not quite figured out what Hunter 1 was doing.

Tonight, he would eliminate Hunter 2. Taking out the second most experienced hunter would greatly increase his odds of survival.

***

The rain was relentless. A veteran of 6 hunts with one win, Hunter 2 should have been prepared. But several days of quiet, combined with the storm, lulled him. At 2:53 a.m., early on Day 9, he was awakened briefly as Prey crashed an 80-pound rock through his tent directly into the side of his skull. After several more strikes, Hunter 2 silently exited this world.

As he had with Hunter 10, Prey retreated to a predetermined spot and observed for the next hour. The only further assault on Hunter 2 was the rain. By 4 a.m., he felt comfortable. He had traveled light. He moved forward, quickly tore down the tent, then used Hunter 2's backpack to secure all his gear. In minutes he was gone, leaving the slaughtered corpse alone in the night.

***

Hunter 1 was always the last to get The Daily Update. He wanted to observe the other hunters. Without reading Day 9's publication, he knew what it would say.

The Daily Update – Day 9

Hunter 2 was discovered early this morning beaten to death with a rock. Substantially all of his gear and supplies were taken.

Standard Footnote: The Daily Update provides daily facts and updates Ogre considers appropriate. It does not opine, speculate, or provide information from prior days.

***

Prey was feeling more confident. Seven down, three to go. He was now better armed. He had 9 bullets and multiple guns in case one jammed. He had the same bows and arrows the hunters had, although he had no idea how to use them. He had plenty of food to last for many days. Water was plentiful on this tropical island. He felt he was mastering another sport even if he would have preferred not to.

***

Day 10. 2:38 a.m. The rain would not end. But Hunter 5 heard something. He was prepared. He had his gun aimed at the tent opening. He was in full gear and wide awake.

***

Prey carefully crept around Hunter 5's campsite. He gently lobbed small rocks and sticks to within 30 feet of the tent. He did this until well after 4:00 a.m. Then he left.

***

At first light, Hunter 5 was out of his tent surveying his campsite. There was no trace of anyone or anything, but the rain could cover a lot. Using experience and caution as a guide, Hunter 5 packed up his campsite and hit the trails. He would find another campsite each night. He wouldn't suffer Hunter 2's fate.

***

Prey watched Hunter 5 move. He then snuggled down for a day of rest.

***

Day 11. The rain continued. Hunter 5 struggled to pitch his tent and keep everything dry. But he finally settled. 2:50 a.m. Prey replayed the prior night. Hunter 5 did as well. He sat up, terrified in his tent, waiting for Prey. At 4:00 a.m. Prey left again, just like the prior night.

***

Prey believed he had appropriately goaded Hunter 5, but he wasn't sure. He watched as Hunter 5 moved. He then settled in for a few hours of sleep before executing his plan. Late in the afternoon, he began slowly, methodically working his way to the newest campsite. He was able to get within 50 feet of the tent. He quietly camouflaged himself, waiting for Hunter 5 to make his move.

***

Hunter 5 thought he knew precisely what he was doing. As daylight faded, he staged his campsite to look like the previous two. Then he quickly stripped out of his bright yellow suit, bathed himself in dirt, and stationed himself just outside of his campsite to wait on his visitor.

***

Prey couldn't believe it. Hunter 5 was ten feet away. He anticipated Hunter 5 trying to lay a trap, but he had no inkling he would make it this easy. Over the prior weeks, and particularly the last several days, he had become adept at slithering silently across the floor of this tropical paradise/madhouse. As dusk turned to darkness, he donned the night vision goggles. Hunter 5 was just waiting, looking toward the campsite, in the opposite direction of Prey. It was fully dark before 10 p.m. The moon had not yet risen. And the rain continued, masking any minor noises. Prey decided to strike now, well before Hunter 5 was expecting his arrival.

As with Hunter 10, Prey buried the knife deep in Hunter 5's neck, reaching around with his left arm to smother any sound. The hunter attempted to swing around, but Prey was too strong. He died quickly.

Again, out of an abundance of caution, Prey backed away and watched. Within the hour, he had packed up substantially all of Hunter 5's gear and headed back to his nicest bunker.

***

Hunter 1 saw that Hunter 5 didn't show up. Interesting. This was getting fun. The Competitor was more accomplished than any he had seen. He must be smart along with athletic. The Daily Update carried no surprises for him today.

The Daily Update – Day 11

Hunter 5 was discovered early this morning with a stab wound to the neck. Substantially all of his gear and supplies were taken. Forecasts show the rain breaking tonight or in the morning with clear skies for the next several days.

Standard Footnote: The Daily Update provides daily facts and updates Ogre considers appropriate. It does not opine, speculate, or provide information from prior days.

***

Prey followed a similar pattern with Hunter 4. On Day 15, at approximately 10:30 p.m., Prey began slithering the 100-plus feet towards the hunter. He would move five to ten feet, pause, survey his target, and continue. He was within ten feet when Hunter 4 turned and looked directly at him. To be accurate, he looked above him since Prey was flat on the ground. But the hunter had heard him or sensed something.

Prey was prepared. First, he lay there quietly for a long time. He knew the moon wouldn't come up for hours, so he could be patient. Eventually, he lobbed a pebble into the campsite. Hunter 4 began searching for the noise, and as he did, Prey moved forward a few feet. He paused and repeated until he was close. As he moved to execute his plan, Hunter 4 sensed him and moved as well. Prey's targeted stab missed, catching Hunter 4 in the back-left shoulder blade. Surprisingly, Hunter 4 only grunted and charged at Prey.

It was no match. In his younger years, Hunter 4 was an elite athlete. But he let ego get the best of him. Rather than being prepared with his gun, he thought he could win a hand-to-hand contest. Prey, on the other hand, had none of this confidence. He came prepared with a large rock. As Hunter 4 charged, Prey braced for the impact, gripping the knife in his dominant hand and rock in his left hand. Prey rolled with the tackle and was immediately on top. He dispatched the billionaire in seconds with little noise.

As he rolled over, breathing hard, he considered his options. On the one hand, they had made some noise, and the rain no longer provided cover. On the other hand, his plan included taking Hunter 4's gear, particularly his food. He would then spend several days and nights in hiding. He would see if he could figure out Hunter 1's routines.

He decided to back further away and wait longer. Virtuous patience was required, as well as preparation. He worked his way slowly to the campsite and quickly loaded the hunter's gear into the hunter's backpack.

***

The first arrow hit him in the left calf. Prey screamed and turned. The second one hit him in the right shoulder. The third one in the gut. And the arrows kept coming. Prey couldn't see where his attacker was in the darkness without his night vision goggles on. More importantly, he did not have a gun in his hand.

Quiet. Hunter 1 waited.

Prey pulled Hunter 4's gun out and chambered a round.

Hunter 1 waited. Eventually, Prey laid down, appearing to pass out.

Hunter 1 waited. Prey was smart. He might just be trying to get him to show himself.

Hunter 1 picked up a small rock and threw it near Prey. No motion. He picked up a larger rock and hit Prey. No motion. Hunter 1 rose, walked to Prey, took the gun out of his hand, kicked him in the side, and poured water from his Yeti on his face.

Prey's eyes opened dimly.

"Well, that was fun, don't you think?" Hunter 1 asked.

"I don't have long. Just tell me how you did it."

"I've followed you off and on since you killed those two idiots on Day 1. This is the ninth time I've played, and I've won three – well, I guess four now. The key is knowing where The Competitor is at all times. Your patterns were easy. So, I could go to The Compound to resupply and get the news and then find you quickly. I know you thought having three separate bunkers was smart, but it just made you move more, and it made it easier to follow you."

"Why?" Prey implored.

Hunter 1 removed his headgear. Prey reacted viscerally.

"Do you know who I am?"

"Of course."

"What is somebody like me supposed to do for fun?"

As Prey began to respond, Hunter 1 sat down on his weakened body, wrapped his gloved hands around his neck, and choked him to death.

***

"That was a good one," Ogre started, raising his glass in a toast.

"Yeah, that kid really brought his A game. It does seem to me the hunters are getting worse," Hunter 1 replied.

Ogre chucked. "You're just getting old. 'The world's going to hell. The kids don't work hard.' It's an age-old story. But this Competitor was just one of the best we have had. That was a great outing."

Hunter 1 finished his drink and headed out. "I have to go. I wasn't planning on taking this long. The twenty-four-hour news cycle will have all sorts of silly speculation about where I am. And the First Lady will be pissed I have been gone so long."

DECAPITATOR 2.0
By William Merrill

"Max stared up at the rollercoaster and reminisced of childhood. He thought about his grandfather, and he thought about the exploding fat man..."

Riders stood in a long line that snaked up to the Red Rooster's loading platform. On the opposite side of the tracks, Carrie and Carl stood waiting for the train to return. Carl's resting biceps stretched his park-issued shirtsleeves as tight as a tourniquet. Carrie looked up the tracks as if the train's return was past due. The Rooster's wet, empty train eased into the station, squeaking then jerking to a stop. Steel gates flung open, and people stepped onto the platform.

Carl and Carrie directed riders to their seats and then lowered safety bars, each locking with a click. A large fella waddled to an open car. The man held the side of the coaster with both hands as he grunted to get his leg over its side. He continued holding on to the car and grunting as he lifted and pulled his other leg in, then eased himself down. Carrie tried to lower the safety bar over him, but his belly prevented it from clicking securely. She whistled to Carl and then motioned him over.

"Why do we even bother?" Carrie sat on the bar, hoping it would lock, but it did not. "The way this guy is jammed in here," she bounced her hundred-and-twenty pounds up and down, listening for a click, "he ain't going anywhere."

"You never read your employee's manual, did you?" Carl stepped from the platform and stood on the safety bar. The obese man grimaced as a roll of his belly pinched between the bar and his knees. "The old timers around here tell me they used to have a lot of flyaways. Made a hell of a mess." Carl squatted, jumped, and landed his hundred-and-ninety pounds on the bar.

The bar clanked as it locked down, followed instantly by high-pitched yelps from the man. He thrashed and kicked and pushed up on the bar with all he had, but the latch was made of very thick steel.

"Shut-up old man." Carl hopped back to the platform. "A dollar more than minimum wage means I don't have to listen to you whine." Carl turned to Carrie. "They'll write you up if you don't' lock 'em in." The man released one hand from the bar and clawed at his chest. Carrie tugged on his left cheek.

"It's not your size," Carl looked at Carrie, "it's your technique. We'll work on it next time."

A middle-aged woman seated near the front of the coaster lit a cigarette. The flash of her lighter caught Carl's eye. Carl turned and jogged up the platform. "Lady! No smoking on this ride."

The middle-aged woman sealed her lips around her cigarette butt, faced Carl, and winked. The tip of her addiction glowed bright red for several seconds. She held in the smoke while flicking her half-burnt cigarette to the platform.

"Didn't you see the signs?" Carl leaned into the car and

checked her safety bar.

The woman blew her smoke into Carl's face. "I saw 'em." She turned and faced forward. "Hell, I even read 'em."

"Enjoy your ride."

A young, redheaded woman in the coaster's control room shifted her hips to match the slow beat of a tune pumping into her earphones. Her upper body was motionless as her lower body glided to one side, eased to a stop, and slid back to the other side. Carl looked at her and gave her a thumbs-up. She pressed the only button on the control panel, a horn blew, hydraulic brakes released, and the train eased out of the pavilion. When the big hill's lift chain engaged, passengers' heads jolted back. On the clanking ride up the incline, some guests shook, some prayed, some writhed in pain, and some held their arms straight up and grinned.

After the train cleared the hill and screams faded to silence, the platform fell quiet. A few moments later, a wet, empty train eased back into the station and squeaked to a stop. The passengers' gates flew open, and riders stepped toward the train.

***

Seven-year-old Max and his grandfather stood at The Red Rooster's entrance. Max backed up to a painting of an oversized rooster. The top of the child's head was well below the chicken's outstretched wing.

"Not quite there yet," Grandpa said.

"I've seen kids younger than me on it."

"As long as this line is, you may be tall enough by the time I get to go." Grandpa reached for the boy's hand. "There're other rides."

The pair, slowed by Grandpa's limp, bumped through a bustling crowd that filled the park's streets and sidewalks. After waiting in line for forty-five minutes, they boarded a little boat that floated through a cave of singing chipmunks and dancing squirrels.

"This is for kids," Max said.

"Oh, come on. What's not to love about singing gophers," Grandpa said. "You'll have plenty of time to be an adult."

***

The pair walked back to the coaster.

"The line isn't as long," Max said. "Can we measure again?"

"How about we get some lunch?"

***

Max and his grandfather sat at a glossy red, plastic table outside of Johnny the Raccoon's Burger Shop. The crowd rushed by as songbirds picked spilled fries from the patio's brick pavers.

"Grandpa, why have you never been on The Rooster?"

"I had better things to do." Grandpa rubbed his abdomen, a nervous habit he developed at war. "Came close, though."

"When Grandma went? You know, she loved it." Max took a drag from his soda. "Why didn't you go when Grandma came?"

"I wanted to." Clear juice oozed from Grandpa's burger as he bit into its center. "Just between me and you…I was chicken."

"Are you still scared of the Rooster?"

"Truth be told, there's not much of anything I'm scared of anymore." Grandpa bit back into his burger but stopped chewing when he crunched something hard. He fished a small chunk of bone out of his mouth and examined it. "For twelve dollars, you'd think they could hire a better butcher."

***

After lunch, Max and his grandfather returned to the coaster.

"The line is much shorter," Max said.

Grandpa scanned the streets and sidewalks. "People are going home earlier and earlier these days. They just gotta get back to their television or their internet and tell their little social media world what a great life they have. Wasting everything God gave them looking at a little screen."

"I don't wanta ever leave."

"We've got time to hit the Rooster later. Let's go do some water rides."

***

Three hours later, Grandpa and Max, dripping wet, approached The Red Rooster's pavilion.

"I guess most everyone went home?" Grandpa said.

"Am I tall enough now?" Max stood on his tiptoes under the chicken.

"Enjoy being young." Grandpa looked at the coaster and then back at Max. "It's my time—you watch me from the fence."

"Have fun, Grandpa."

Grandpa hugged Max and entered the Rooster's pavilion through a turnstile. He limped through a maze of ropes and posts and finally to the coaster's loading station. Grandpa stood behind a large man who was sweating and grimacing. The big man held his upper right abdomen with one hand and leaned against a column with his other hand. A wet, empty train rolled into the station and squeaked to a stop.

"Step forward and enter the seat in front of you," Carl shouted.

Grandpa boarded and lowered his safety bar until it clicked into place.

The large man attempted to enter a middle car but stopped when Carl yelled, "Hey, you'll throw our balance off. Get in the back car."

The man turned and limped down the dock, still grasping his abdomen.

Carl looked at Carrie. "You wanta see if you can do this one?"

"I guess it's 'big guy' day at the park." Carrie turned toward the back of the coaster.

"Every day is here." Carl pushed and locked the safety bar over a teenage girl. He saw a cell phone in her hand. "No electronics allowed. Hand it to me." Carl leaned down and snatched the phone from her. "I hope that text message was important."

Carrie watched as the large man struggled to lift his leg over the car. "Sir, you need to get in. Now!" Carrie marched to the back of the coaster. "Move your ass."

When the man's foot touched the wet vinyl seat, he slipped and crashed into his seat. Carrie lowered his safety bar, but it wasn't even close to latching. She backed up seven steps, sprinted across the platform, and leaped. She landed on the bar with both feet, squashing the man's belly flat and locking the bar in place. The man screamed and thrashed about.

"Shut up," Carrie said. She hopped from the car to the platform, leaned over, put both hands on her knees, and raised her head. "How'd I do?"

"Couldn't have done it better myself." Carl stared down her shirt.

The redhead shouted from the booth. "Don't you two have a job to do?"

Carl turned back to the train and walked the length of the platform, looking for contraband and checking each car's safety bar. As he got to Grandpa's car, he leaned down and grabbed the bar. "Cancer keeps you skinny." He tugged up. "Makes my job a hell of a lot easier."

Grandpa snatched Carl's wrist and pulled him close. "I took

Vietnamese shrapnel so you could get a thrill looking at that girl. The least you could do is greet me with respect." Grandpa released. "Right now, you're too ignorant to realize what this all means."

Carl pulled his hand back, "Have a good ride, sir." He looked at the redhead in the booth and gave her a thumbs-up. As the coaster eased out of the station, Carl thought about Grandpa. For the first time in his life, he really thought about The Rooster. He stopped himself from that line of thinking by shaking it off and then fantasizing about Carrie.

***

As Max peered at the tracks through a chain link fence, a tall man carrying a cane and wearing a tuxedo and a top hat approached him.

"You got a friend on The Rooster?" The man in the top hat said.

"My grandpa."

"Well then, this is a special day, and I have a special place for young men watching their grandparents ride."

The man led Max along a path that wound around and behind the coaster to a crowded aluminum bleacher. The stands overlooked a straight section of track at the bottom of the coaster's final big hill. An enormous Lexan panel allowed the audience an unobstructed view.

The man with the top hat stood between the viewing panel and the bleachers. He slapped the giant window with his cane. "Ladies and gentlemen, little boys and little girls, as we speak, your friends and relatives are being strapped in for the ride of the Universe." He tipped his top hat.

"I give you the most exhilarating roller coaster in the WORLD, The Reeeeeeeeeeed ROOSTER!" The man pointed his cane at the crowd. "She'll throw your hair back, she'll tingle your guts, she'll chatter your teeth, she'll make you scream, and even rattle your bones the same as she rattles the timbers that hold her together. By the time you hit that final drop, you'll pray for its end and wish it wasn't over at the same time... then BAM, you're done."

A young girl raised and waved her hand.

"We have a question from a beautiful young lady—yes, ma'am?"

She pointed to a wedged-shaped metal blade that hung low across the track. "What's that?"

"You, young lady, are very observant. Its official name is The Decapitator 2.0, but here at the park, we have many names for it. Some call it the rooster's claw, The 2.0, The Big D, The eliminator, and my personal favorite, 'your inheritance on a stick." The man in the top hat pointed his cane at the young girl. "No matter its name, you should know that it truly is a marvel of modern engineering."

"It's just a big razor blade," said a woman sitting in the middle of the stands.

"Oh no, no, no...it's so much more." He pointed his cane at the woman. "Ma'am, at sixty miles an hour, bones can dull ordinary steel in less than a day. The 2.0 is made of a composite alloy that can be sharpened to the finest point. It'll still be slicing and dicing long after you and I are dead and gone." He scanned the crowd. "Any of you remember the eighties? When men wore those thick gold necklaces?"

Several in the crowd nodded.

"Turns out, a lot of 'em were just gold coated. All that cheap metal ground our old blade dull in just forty or fifty passes. By early afternoon, we were doing more tearing than slicing." The man in the top hat scratched the back of his neck. "There was an incident in eighty-nine—last run of the day. The 1.0 was so dull that the train stopped dead—halfway through a gentleman from Minnesota. Damn thing lodged right in the guy's ribs. Big strong guy...I remember it like it was yesterday—he was wearing a pink jacket." The man in the top hat cackled. "Needless to say, those passengers riding behind him were not a joyful lot."

"What did you do?" The woman said.

"We hired the best engineers in the world, and they gave us The Decapitator 2.0."

"No!" The woman said. "How did they—"

"Darlin' they just blowtorched the 1.0 apart and sold the pieces sold as scrap."

"I don't care about the stupid blade. What happened to the riders in the back."

"Here at the park, we do care about the blade, and you should too. The loss of the 1.0 was a big deal." The man in the top hat smiled. "The passengers in the back certainly weren't going anywhere."

"Did they have to go again?"

"Without a blade? Now that would be pointless—"

"How did you—"

"Maintenance just sent out a guy with a mallet. It was a big damn mess, for sure. Worst yet was that Management had to pay a whole bunch of overtime."

"How often do you sharpen it?" A man in the back said.

"That's a very good question. The answer is, we don't...and that's what makes 2.0 a marvel. You see, a laser keeps it at the perfect height, and our engineer came up with the idea of putting a Japanese whetstone on the front and rear edge of the train. Now, we sharpen and slice all in one pass. It's certified, guaranteed, or our money back."

"What do you do with the riders?"

The man in the top hat chuckled. "Well, we don't really call them riders at that point. We dispose of the parts responsibly. You see, this park is completely self-sufficient, environmentally responsible, and nothing goes to waste." The man in the top hat took in a big breath as if smelling coffee first thing in the morning. "I can tell you that our flowers don't stay this beautiful without a little help from our guests." He turned his head and listened for the coaster. "Folks, folks...they're climbing the big hill."

***

As the coaster lurched up the first hill, Grandpa could see that the park's giant parking lot was still full.

***

"A man sitting on the top bleacher raised his hand, "Do they know what's coming?"

"That, my fellow Earth traveler, is what makes The Rooster the most exciting ride in the world." He pointed his cane at the peak of the last hill.

"As Grandma or Grandpa—Management makes us say both so as not to offend— as she slowly rolls over this last big hill, she gets a good long view of the 2.0, and if that doesn't scare the wits out of her," he raised his eyebrows, "we've added a little surprise."

"I love surprises," said a young girl sitting near Max. "What is it?"

"Only Management knows…and, of course," he chucked, "those guests going over the hill. But we all know they won't tell."

As the coaster accelerated through the first drop, screams shifted by the Doppler Effect filled the park.

"Oh, come on," a woman said. "What's the surprise?"

"Okay, okay—I can tell you this…Management painted a message on the top of the blade."

"What's it say?"

The man in the top hat pretended not to hear the question.

"What does it say."

"Lady, I don't know. The only ones that can see it are the riders coming over the last drop."

"Oh, come on, you know."

"All I can tell you is that you'll be able to see their change in expression the instant they read it."

***

As the coaster contorted through the first trough, it pressed Grandpa into his seat. Max said to the man in the top hat,

"Does it hurt?"

"How the hell should I know?"

***

As the coaster flew over the second hill, Grandpa felt nearly a second of weightlessness. He held his hands straight up and smiled as the train flew around a sharp curve that wound into a spiral.

***

A man sitting on the back of the bleachers said, "Has anyone ever made it through alive?"

"No," The man in the top hat said. "That's all the time we have for questions. Sit back, relax, and enjoy their ride."

***

The coaster snaked out of the spiral and shot up a steep incline nearly as tall as the first hill. Grandpa kept his hands up as the train crested, then plunged vertical and into a tunnel.

***

The young girl sitting near Max saw a tear in Max's left eye. She slid next to him, reached over, and clasped his hand. "It's okay—your grandfather is happy now."

***

The coaster flew out of the backside of the tunnel, galloped over four bunny hills, through a curve to the left, another curve to the right, and slowed as it approached the final hill.

***

The young girl extended a corndog under Max's nose. "You can have it."

"No thank you."

***

Grandpa kept his hands up as a second lift chain engaged and slowly pulled the cars up a steep incline.

***

"You'll feel better if you eat something." The young girl stroked the inside of Max's palm with her fingertips. "Do it for me."

"Okay." Max took the corndog and bit off its top. "Thank you," he said while chewing.

***

As the coaster crested and the blade came into view, Grandpa dropped his hands. When he read the words painted across the top of the blade, his eyes widened, his mouth dropped open, and his expression froze.

***

The man in the top hat slapped the viewing panel with his cane, "Ladies and Gentlemen, this rooster is about to CROW!"

The Red Rooster made its final drop and roared past the

bleachers. The 2.0 caught most passengers, including Grandpa, just below their ribs. The wedge-shaped blade sent heads with torsos twenty feet above the tracks. The smaller female halves flew as high as thirty feet. When the crowd heard what sounded like scores of steel BBs peppering the viewing panel, they jerked back and gasped. Slime-encased pellets stuck to the Lexan and oozed to the ground.

"OH GOOD GOD!" the man in the top hat yelled. He looked at the tracks, spun back to the crowd, and then back to stare at the viewing panel. "Ladies and gentlemen, you—you have—you have just witnessed the rarest of the rare. I've been here thirty years, and I've never—"

"What happened?" said a man in the back.

"We call it...we call it the shotgun. Hell, I thought it was a myth." The man removed his top hat and scratched his head. "A thousand variables have to be just right. The passenger has to be seated in the last car. He has to be slumped over...the gallbladder at the perfect height. The 2.0 has caught it at the exact angle—just shave the top off—a few millimeters out either way, and it doesn't work." The man with the top hat rubbed his temples between his forefinger and thumb. "It has to be full of stones, they have to be the right size, the wind has to be directly toward us, but not too fast. Hell, the safety bar has to squeeze with the exact pressure—it's—it's a Goddamn miracle." He retrieved a phone from his pocket and pointed to a woman sitting in the middle of the stands. "Ma'am—ma'am, would you mind taking a picture of me in front of the pattern?"

***

The train eased over a hill, around a curve, and stopped on a straightaway. A section of track, slightly longer than the train, slowly rotated the cars upside down. Intestines unfurled and swung in the breeze while blue-veined organs fell from their holds to a growing pyramid below. With a loud mechanical pop, all of the safety bars released, and legs still attached to abdomens fell to the pile, landing with a wet slap. The Red Rooster rotated upright, eased down the track through rings of high-pressure water jets, and rolled back to the station.

***

Seventy-two years later, Max waited to board The Red Rooster. Max stared up at the rollercoaster and reminisced of childhood. He thought about his grandfather, and he thought about the exploding fat man. He wondered if he would see them again, he wondered what was written across the top of the 4.0, but mostly, he wondered how bad it was going to hurt.

LIFE GIVER
BY DEREK WAUTLET

Pebbles were thrown up into the afternoon sunshine as Life Giver rolled down the abandoned street. His pace never changed, a constant speed that showed no sense of true urgency, nor did it signify he was hesitant to reach his final destination. The hard rubber treads wrapped around steel wheels allowed him to traverse almost any terrain.

He released an array of different beeps and boops, signifying he was taking the surrounding area's temperature, air quality, and chemical reading. Once again, it was inhospitable. The temperature was mild and could sustain life, but the chemicals present from the last bioweapon's release made the air toxic. Creating a mammal here would either mean instant death or - if Life Giver underestimated the lethalness - a lifetime of suffering. The thing it spawned here would bring him no closer to his ultimate goal, as it would be infertile.

The dusty road was lined with the skeletons of once great human achievement. He passed a museum that was once full of artwork, books, and historical artifacts. It had cataloged many of the great events in the nation's history. Now it only cataloged but one thing: destruction. A once bustling office building serving as a commercial hub in the city had been turned to rubble. An array of automobiles that had evolved from the once great innovation of Henry Ford now appeared as lifeless hunks of metal.

Hours passed, and the solar panels on Life Giver's back rose off his body and dipped forward a few degrees. The flawless design follows the sun as it moves across the sky and captures every ounce of daylight energy. As the sun fell below the horizon, the panels rested once again against Life Giver's frame. He continued traveling through the night with equal purpose as in the day.

By the next morning, Life Giver had reached the rocky highlands surrounding the once prosperous human settlement. His solar-powered engine protested with a screech now as he had to work harder to make it up the sloping foothills. The small bushes littering the foothills here were coated with a layer of thick pink dust. The aftermath of whatever chemical was most recently used to exterminate the population here.

The wilderness began to increase in elevation, and the surface he was traversing became rockier. Eviscerated versions of quaking aspens dotted the side of the mountain. No leaves were present on the trees, and the bark was charred a dark brown. They appeared like a starving climbing party, naively thinking a glorious feast awaited them at the top. They would gorge themselves on an assortment of meats and fresh fruit but never truly be full again.

***

After days of climbing, Life Giver approached the summit of the highest peak yet. The dead aspens were thick here, with an occasional rock structure jutting out. The built-in odometer read

14,100 feet. A red warning appeared flashing in front of Life Giver's visual interface. It signified that the power level was running low, and he would need to stop and recharge, or his systems would begin to malfunction. Two titanium arms emerged from the top of Life Giver's body and planted themselves on the ground in front of him. They began pulling him along, assisting with the final steep ascent.

Once on the mountain top, Life Giver's odds of finding a habitable zone drastically increased. A fresh water source lay 500 feet below, nestled in the mountains. It was a long and narrow lake that seemed to stretch on indefinitely. The water was blue from a distance but surely had some deadly chemical content present. Most other lakes and streams had dried up after one of the many explosions. If a human was here, they would surely celebrate this moment and take a photograph, but Life Giver was in desperate need of a recharge. He entered hibernation mode and allowed the solar panels to do the work.

Upon awakening, Life Giver rode down the other side of the peak towards the lake. He lost his traction and began sliding down the mountain more than once. Soon enough, he arrived at the blue mass. Pink particles floated on top of the surface, but it looked unusually clean for a lake post radioactive fallout. Life Giver inserted a metallic blue needle into the lake to take a quick measurement and then continued moving along the valley.

The lake stretched for a little over two miles before coming to an end. A creek exited from the east side of the lake, and Life

Giver calculated a potentially beneficial outcome as he approached. The water flowed through a collection of rocks at the end of the lake and then began to descend fast and widen down the mountain. If algae and other microorganisms still existed on those rocks, then there was a chance the water could be drinkable.

Life Giver approached the creek and stuck in its tendrils, but it was too far away. He began to climb down some of the rocks, using his metallic arms for assistance. One of the boulders it had grabbed moved, and his robotic form swayed. Another boulder moved, and Life Giver lost his balance, splashing right into his newfound hope.

The creek continued to become clearer as Life Giver bobbed up and down on the surface. The need to steady himself and return to the shore became less urgent as he began to realize the increasing odds of there being a hospitable zone further into the valley. Life Giver's cylindrical head began rotating, the spider-like eyes absorbing everything around it. All of the measurement devices were activated and began producing multitudes of positive readouts.

Green and yellow numbers began pouring out to Life Giver's optical interface rather than the red that always appeared before. This could be a hospitable zone - or the closest to a hospitable zone that his travels had brought him to yet. The two titanium arms once again emerged from the top of Life Giver's intelligence unit. They stabbed into the earth to his right side and pulled his metallic body out of the river full of hope.

As soon as he reached the surface, he retracted the working

arms and inserted two metallic blue needles into the earth. Another hopeful sign - Life Giver's readouts indicated some micro bacteria had survived the fallout. That means the opportunity for fungus and plant growth. That means a viable source of food for his young organisms to get their start on. Then he could work on producing a population of prey animals for them to feed on.

Life Giver continued moving through the forest. The valley floor and dead trees were still coated in pink dust, but it wasn't as thick as outside. The surrounding mountains must have blocked the effects of the explosions, and the elevation prevented the biochemicals from getting a chance to spread. The perfect combination of environmental factors led to this oasis being formed.

He retracted his sensors from the earth and began moving further down the valley, parallel to the creek. Suddenly a blurry figure flashed in front of Life Giver's visual interface. Then another blur, then another. Suddenly there was a crash, and a large crack appeared on the screen. Then another crash, and the world went dark for a while.

***

"The confederate probably dropped these robotic soldiers to exterminate any of the survivors of the blasts. Those bastards always had to be so thorough." Life Giver heard a female voice say.

"I don't think so," another said.

"Not a chance. The confederate barely dropped their last bioweapons before we evaporated their continent. There's no way they would have time to get these bots through," a man's baritone voice said.

Life Giver's visual interface began to boot up, but everything appeared black around him. They must have somehow tied the intelligence unit in its closed position.

"So where exactly," said a gravelly voice and then the sound of someone spitting, "do you think it came from?"

"I think it's one of ours. Maybe a scouting bot searching for signs of life. Maybe it could even help us search for food," said the baritone voice.

"Are you willing to bet your life on it? I think we should have destroyed this thing outside. Jerome get the axe-"

"Hey!" a feminine voice interjected. "Listen to what Mark is saying. This thing could be valuable."

"I'm not saying we release it. I'm just saying ask it some questions and see how it responds. Robots that are part of the continental alliance are programmed to answer all fairly posed questions," said Mark.

"Fine, do it," said the gravelly voice.

Life Giver heard footsteps approaching him. They stopped, and he could sense a biological lifeform within a few feet.

"Hello." Mark's voice sounded very close. "My name is Mark. As it is your duty to the alliance, answer all of my questions courteously and without question. Will you comply?"

"Yes, I will comply." Life Giver activated his sound box and language system for the first time in nearly three months. He heard some brief shuffling, and then all was quiet again.

"What is your ID verification code?"

"L-I-F-E-G-V-R-7-7-3-2," Life Giver said, speaking each of the characters slowly and carefully.

"And what is your designated purpose?"

"Purpose 1: Survive human doomsday event. Purpose 2: Locate a habitable zone. Purpose 3: Use biological material to create viable human offspring. Purpose 4: Raise offspring to build back the ideal human civilization."

Life Giver heard a gasp from one of the women in the group. Another person clapped their hands together.

"Finally, salvation is here," one person said.

"No more worrying. We have alliance AI technology here to help us now," another person said.

"I wouldn't be so sure," the gravelly voice spoke, and Life Giver heard footsteps approaching once again. "Where were you produced?"

"Alliance Depot 392, Northern Continent Division."

"Who gave you your instructions?"

"Colonel Jeffrey Kolto."

"If we release you, what will you do?"

"Take all necessary action to build and preserve human life."

"What does that entail?"

"Growing and creating food, providing shelter, instructing on behavioral essentials, protecting at all costs."

"Sounds all nice and convenient, but I still don't trust it. This thing could easily be a confederate soldier bot that is trying to trick us with false information."

"Don't be foolish, Eugene. No soldier bots are designed like that. They aren't capable of deceit. If it was a confederate droid, it would have come through the forest with its guns out as soon as it sensed life. Or it would have self-destructed as soon as we started questioning it."

"Don't you call me a damn fool." Eugene's voice grew louder. "I ain't ever trusted no damn machine, and I'm not about to start now. We've been doing fine on our own, eating snails from the creek and bulbs of those plants. If you're right about those fruit trees, they'll be growing back soon, and we'll have enough food to survive."

"We're barely living now, Eugene. That food isn't more than 100 calories a day, and for all we know, it could be killing us if it is infected with the chemicals too. This AI could help us survive. It can teach us how to find viable food and protect us in case there are still dangerous things out there. We need to release it."

Life Giver opened a small hatch and projected an image of the Alliance emblem on whatever surface was above him. He heard more gasps from the people around him.

"It must be one of ours."

"A confederate bot couldn't be programmed like that."

"Now you have to see Eugene. Alliance property can be trusted."

"Fine, remove the rocks and the ties."

Life Giver felt objects slowly being removed from around his steel form. The humans were working slowly but diligently. Then he felt the tie around his optical and intelligence units being removed. He regained the freedom over his senses, and his optical unit rose from his body.

He scanned his surroundings, observing the lifeforms around him. Nine humans loomed at the same level of his optical unit. They appeared to have taken him into their shelter, a damp cave with a small torch in one corner and a small amount of sunlight visible through the entrance at the other corner. Their bodies all appeared very thin and ragged. Their faces were covered in dirt and soot.

The largest frame he assumed to be Mark, and the grizzled old man at his side he assumed to be Eugene. A large jug of clear liquid in the corner that Life Giver assumed was being used to collect water from the creek.

As Life Giver scanned his surroundings, he continued with his calculations of potential outcomes of Purpose 4. Raising humans to build back the ideal human civilization meant that, without question, the humans had to follow his orders. They had to behave how he intended them to behave. They had to resolve conflicts how he suggested they resolve conflicts. Had to form governments how he instructed them to form governments.

Life Giver observed all of the ribs sticking out of skeleton-like frames. The faces drained of emotion and feeling. The hatred present on Eugene and his son's faces. The neverending suffering that these people endured. Surely they could never build back the world he intended. They had seen far too much. The world they intended to build would be survival at whatever cost and surely wouldn't involve utopian idealism.

The calculations of Purpose Number Four led to only one potential outcome in this hospitable zone. The group cheered as Life Giver rose up to his full size. Treads moving towards them.

"Our savior is here!"

"Where should we look for food?"

"How can we design a pulley system to bring in the fishing materials?"

"How can we bring the forest back to life?"

The questions kept coming, and Life Giver activated his weapons system. The laser weapon emerged from his back, and the crowd was silenced.

"What is th-" Mark's questions stopped as the automatic rounds turned his body into a ragged mess of flying flesh and blood. Blood-curdling screams emanated from the group as they watched their fellow survivors sliced to pieces by the red lasers on Life Giver's back. The weapon circled the cave, eviscerating every organism in sight. The walls were littered with the remains of Life Giver's capturers. Soon, all was silent, and Purpose Number Four's greatest threats had been eliminated.

Life Giver began cleaning every square inch of the cave and collecting the human remains in the rocky prison he had been locked in. They would make the perfect fertilizer for use in growing his garden that would be used to produce the food for his ideal human civilization.

Once the shelter was prepared, and the food was ready, he would begin the creation of his humans capable of completing Purpose Number Four in this habitable zone. He was very excited to meet them.

THE BOOK OF ALL BOOKS
By Darrell Grant

Months had passed, and I had spent most of it trying to write a book. I had the hope that every writer has had in the past and present, that the effort would pay off, and it turned out to be a great book. I believe I had not written a word. Not a single word had been put on paper, it was a writer's block of all writer's blocks, and when I got tired of waiting to get past it, I gave up.

As a joke to myself, I put papers together, as empty as they were, into a blinder, made a cover for it, and for no known reason I knew of at the time, I titled it.

"This you see if you want to see." Then I closed the book and called my friend John. I told him that I had finished my book. He made me feel good about our friendship because even from the phone, I could tell he was jumping with joy for me.

He said, "let's go out and bring it with you." I agreed, said OK, and then met up with him with the papers in a binder that I called a book

As we dined, he suddenly shouted rather loud, "Come on, man, show me the book." So, I pulled out the book with its nice cover. He looked at it, and he told me that I was probably a better artist than a writer. I laughed as I handed it to him, but I was thinking that he was probably right.

He opened it and started glancing over the book quickly. He was going through the pages looking up and down, turning the pages faster and faster. At first, I just sat there watching with amazement but then I figured he was now turning the tables, and the joke was now on me. He continued, and I remember saying out loud, "What the hell." And saying to myself that he was playing his role better than I was playing mine

After a few minutes, I laughed and said, "Yes, it is empty, it is my novel, and it's a damn joke."

He seemed to not hear or was ignoring what I said, and at that very second, he just started crying, and then the crying became mixed with smiles of joy. Then he seriously and shockingly looked up and said ... "I'll take two."

Little did I know then that that was the beginning of the road that would lead to the book becoming the best selling novel of all novels.

Even though, at that moment in time, I just knew or thought John was just messing with me, I still decided to play the same joke again, only this time on my publisher, maybe because I was probably losing my mind. I didn't know the answer to that for sure, but that didn't stop me from showing up at his office and telling him I had a book. I pulled it out as I was sitting myself down and laughing at the same time. He looked at me and asked me if this meant that I was now into writing comedies. Then he asked to see it but not before reminding me that I had been trying to write another book for a long time and he didn't think he could carry me much longer.

He had tried to help by advancing me money, hoping that I

would do something, anything, even short stories, which I did, and they were wonderful but not what he really wanted. I knew he would soon have to let me go. Business was business. He grabbed the book out of my hand and began to go though it faster and faster as my friend did. He, too, started crying and then smiling before crying again and then ending up with what I believed were more smiles of joy.

He looked through that book as though he, too, was seeing the words on those pages that had only been seen by one other, my friend John Nelson.

He said, "This has got to be a novel for all novels. We will go to print, we will go to print now."

What had started off as a joke was now beyond my understanding but would turn out to be financially beneficial and remain a mystery to me for a long time.

He really did print what to me at the time was 450 blank pages of nothing, and every time somebody that could also see the words read that book, they had the same response, they cried, smiled with happiness, and cried as they read the words in the book. Again, the words that I had not seen. It became the biggest bestselling book of all time. It truly was a novel of all novels, and as strange as it all was, I stopped questioning what others were seeing.

I lived my life in luxury for years while sometimes thinking about the words that others had seen. Even though I didn't really ever question it all as deeply as I should have, I did sometimes wonder. I wondered how it could be that I couldn't see. To be honest, I also said to myself at times, "I don't care," and that's because sometimes money can be blinding.

I will admit that sometimes wondering left me with an eerie feeling that was void of an answer, but the book seemed to bring joy to the world along with Bestsellers lists and interviews. When asked once by an interviewer how I had come about to write this book, I said honestly, "I don't know. I couldn't tell even if I wanted too." It always brought laughter from the audience, and the book went on and on. I never wrote another book, and whenever I asked somebody who had read the book what they liked and if they could explain to me what they thought the book was all about, they simply answered, "You know, you should know, or you will know."

One year later, after the first publication, I pulled out the original book I had made, which by now I had encased. I said to myself, "I'm going to look at this once again," because somehow, someway, I wanted and had to know what I had done, what I was part of, what I had brought to this world that caused tears, joy, happiness and hope to others while for some reason it was all being excluded from me.

I opened it in my new office, but on the same lucky old desk I had put it together that night. I stared at the first page over and over again, but I still saw nothing at all. Then after about three minutes, my life changed, and I saw and found all the answers I ever wanted and would ever need.

Down on that page, writing began to appear. I could only see just a few words on the first page of the book, and for whatever reason, they would forever be the only words I would ever be able to see in that book. This gave me a sense of enlightenment and an understanding that I was just an instrument in something I should never again question.

The words that appeared to me were, "I Am the Almighty ... Cry and Rejoice for you have been chosen to see thy words in this book.... the second book of all books."

RUNNING
By Henry Valerio

"Somebody is at the door, honey," the lady told her husband.

"Yeah, if he continues knocking that way, he'll break the door into pieces. God damn it!" her husband answered back and walked towards the front door. "Can you hear it? This person will get to know me soon. You'll see," he added. He took a Glock 42, with his left hand, from the elegant console table. Then the husband opened the door angrily with his right hand while hiding the gun behind the front door.

"Good evening, sir! I'm so sorry to bother you, but..." the stranger greeted.

"You're bleeding! What happened?" The husband interrogated and immediately hid his small weapon inside his pants and stepped forward to check if there was someone else around. Finally, he helped the visitor to come inside the house.

"Jesus Christ! A young man in trouble! Poor fellow!" the wife exclaimed.

The stranger fainted.

***

Where am I at? I recall now..."

The stranger got out of the guest room and went downstairs.

He heard some noise in the kitchen.

"Good morning!" he said timidly.

"Hello there! Good morning!" the lady said in a friendly way.

"I hope you feel better this morning. You passed out last night. You were kind of weak, I guess. I cleaned you up and dressed your wounds," the husband explained. He was a strong man; he looked tough, like a Marlboro man on TV.

"Thank you, sir. I thank you both. By the way, my name is Vince Edwards."

"I am Marvin, and she is my wife, Amber."

"It's a real pleasure to meet both of you. I was lucky to find your house in the mountains last night, the only light around. It's an isolated place!" Vince added.

"Would you like to join us for breakfast? I have everything ready and set. You must be hungry! Moreover, you need some protein to recover yourself," Amber offered.

"Of course, thank you, ma'am. Thank both of you for your hospitality."

They took breakfast without talking much. Amber and Marvin looked at each other occasionally.

"Ma'am, you're an excellent cook! You are a lucky man, sir. A nice and beautiful wife and a nice and beautiful house!"

"Thank you, young man," Amber smiled.

"Thanks. However, this is our refuge in the mountains," Marvin explained.

"Our love nest," his wife interrupted to cover Marvin's last words.

"She's right. We live in the city. Any time we need a break, we come here."

"I see. That's wonderful."

"Listen, Vince, I know it's hard to tell things to strangers, but…"

"I am a stranger, and I can be a dangerous fellow. I understand, sir. You, I mean, both of you, are wondering why or how I ended up here, right?"

"That's correct."

Marvin and Amber looked at each other and then looked at Vince.

"It's a long story!"

"I LOVE long stories!" Amber said childishly.

Both men smiled.

Vince concluded he needed to trust his host and hostess; maybe they could help him fix things before calling 911.

"Where should I begin? Let me see… I know! It all started when I was in high school."

Marvin was surprised. He didn't expect it was that long ago. Amber was happy because she realized it was going to be a long story, indeed.

"My high school was not controlled by the school authorities, you know, it was ruled by a senior student who was a drug dealer. His father was a mafia godfather, at least, I was told. His father controlled all illegal businesses in town," Vince commenced his story.

As soon as Amber listened to Vince's words, she looked her husband straight in the eye.

"And it was a problem but, sincerely, NOT my problem. I'm not the police, you know. I was a senior, too. The thing was that I asked a girl to be my girlfriend, and that kid, Samuel, had been in love with her all along. I didn't know that. Suddenly, I became Sam's enemy."

Marvin saw Amber this time.

"It was our last year at school. I thought it was not going to be a big deal to date..."

"Mary," the lady interrupted.

"Wow! How did you know her name?"

Marvin tapped the kitchen table softly with his fist, and then he was the one who looked at his wife straight in the eye.

Amber blushed and added, "I guessed it. It's a very common name."

"You're right, ma'am. I think it's a common name. Anyway, this guy, Samuel, tried to make my life a living hell; well, he had his friends, and I had nobody to protect me since everybody was afraid of his father's powerful hand."

"But last night, you were hurt!" Marvin indirectly asked.

"Oh, yes, sir, you are right, back to the point. Samuel has ALWAYS hated me since that year on. My parents moved me to another school and asked me to stop seeing Mary. So, I didn't see Sam for a long time."

"Until last night, I guess," Marvin said.

"Nope… 2 days ago, on Wednesday. I was grocery shopping when Samuel and his friends came for some cigarettes and a six-pack beer. Fortunately, they didn't see me."

"So?" Amber asked.

"The cashier asked them for the money because they were about to leave the place. Sam told the cashier if he knew who he was. The guy told Samuel he didn't care. I am Salvatore Romano; that's what Samuel said and shot the cashier to death."

"I recall it now. It was on the TV news."

"You are right, ma'am. It was breaking news."

Both spouses were genuinely interested in Vince's story.

"Go on," Marvin ordered.

Vince thought it was kind of rude, but he continued his story. "Samuel, well, Salvatore, I didn't know that was his real name, I left the store after taking all the money from the cash register."

"And what does it have to do with you, young man?" the lady asked.

"The police came and interrogated all clients separately. I was the only MORON who identified Sam and his accomplices. The others told the police officers they didn't remember shit! Pardon my language."

Marvin excused himself to go to another room. Vince thought he needed the restroom.

"So, Vince, you are the guy missing, the one the police are looking for. I also watched it on TV news."

"You're right, ma'am. I've been running away from him and his father's men all this time because they don't want a living witness, of course."

"I understand," the lady said.

"Sam, Salvatore, found my apartment. He and his 4 partners in crime tried to kill me yesterday when I was starting my car to go to work. I got shot for the first time, only once. Nonetheless, I was able to escape. I ran over a couple of his men... I'm not sure if I killed them or not. I just drove my car out of the city."

"You did. Both of them died. It was on TV, too," the lady explained.

"OH... MY... GOD! That's too bad! The rest of them followed me and shot me again. My car died. I had to walk into the woods. They were shooting like crazy in the forest. I hid behind a tree, and I knocked out another man by hitting him with a thick branch in his face. I kept running till I saw a train station; I got on an Amtrak train that was leaving. I jumped off the train the first chance I had because Samuel's last man was also able to get on the train. He jumped off, too... he didn't make it. He broke his neck. I ran a lot more. I saw a light on this mountain, and here I am."

Marvin came back to the kitchen. Vince turned his head to the left and felt the butt of a shotgun, a blackout for a couple of hours.

***

"Samuel, I mean, Salvatore! What are you doing here? What is this?"

Vince was tied to a chair in the backyard.

"Somebody HELP ME."

"You can shout, go ahead. Nobody will hear you; remember, we are in the mountains," Marvin observed.

Marvin continued his speech. "Allow me to introduce ourselves properly. My full name is Marvino Romano. As you already know, Amber Romano is my wife… and this is Salvatore Romano, our treasure and sole surviving son. In our line of business, the death rate is extremely high, and we do whatever it takes to keep the family traditions. I'm sorry to say."

"Oh darling, you seem to be a kind person, but…" Amber added.

"Therefore, this is a farewell, Vince. God, I hate this guy!" Salvatore said at the end.

Then he pointed the shotgun at Vince's head and shot.

MISS DOOM N' GLOOM
BY WILL HERSHEY

The electric blue eyes that she always protected and loved were being pulled away from her, pupils smaller and smaller as they dragged him farther and farther away. Meaty hands wrapped around his bony shoulders and threw him behind the thick glass window. I held Father's reassuring palms with my tiny hands as the red dust spit from spinning treads, headed towards The Laboratory.

Streaks of sound reverberate off the walls from that stupid little alarm clock as Ari's eyes shot open. Another night. Another fucking night she'd had that dream. Another fucking night that the sadistic psychopaths came and took her brother away to be used in some sort of sick experiment. And, of course, another morning where she wakes up and stares into his unforgiving eyes on her nightstand.

The memory was pressed deep into her subconscious, causing night terrors nearly every time she closed her weary eyes. But, like every other day, there comes a point where it's time to shut the brain up, get out of a warm cocoon of self-pity, and put those feet on the cold stone floor. There is always the motivation to also turn off that stupid alarm.

She lifted herself out of her all too comfortable bed, her head feeling like a weight against the pillow. She cracked her neck and faced the nightstand. She gently stroked her brother's face, taking a moment to appreciate his innocence once again before starting her day. She turned and began her daily routine: brushing her teeth, combing those pesky knots out of her hair, and haphazardly shoving herself into her work jumpsuit.

Ari then walked to a kitchen and shook out the dry, cheap cereal out of its box into her glass bowl. She put two pieces of bread into the toaster, grabbed an empty glass on the shelf, and put it on the counter. She stopped, turning on her little government-issued radio to hear the news for the day. She took the carton of orange juice out of the fridge and poured it directly over the small pieces of granola, slowly corrupting each individual piece with an unnatural combination of flavors as her mind drifted to the crackly voices blaring through the radio speakers, "Good morning all and welcome to your daily M.C.R. news update. I'm your host Ziles Chaundry, here to start off your morning with a fresh dose of science! We have a very special guest: Dr. Xavier Thominson, The Chief Scientist of The Laboratory…"

Ari's hands stiffened around her spoon as it filled with the concoction in her bowl, her teeth grinding together. "You son of a bitch," she whispered as she took her first bite. Granola and orange juice sprayed across the kitchen counter as she spit it out in surprise. "What the hell, Ari."

"But first, I'm happy to give you a weather update on this surprisingly pleasant Monday morning…"

"Yeah. Pleasant," Ari muttered, wiping down her previously clean white countertop, pushing soggy granola into the metal trash can.

"I know that you folks had to spend this weekend indoors due to the dust storms rolling through downtown. There wasn't any life lost as most citizens followed the protocols, and only minor property damage has been noted. This week will be substantially better! Feel free to step outside, wearing those lovely masks of yours, and throw the old pigskin around with your kids or maybe get in some of that subterranean gardening you've been putting off! We've got a temperate readout of..."

Ari glanced at the clock. *Ah fuck. Time to skedaddle.* She grabbed the tattered backpack (the one with Leo written in big letters on one of the straps) off the stool. She shoved in a banana and a half-eaten sub from yesterday as she naturally tuned back into the scraggly audio of that little radio, "... and doctor, we've heard consistent coverage in the media these days about your trials. Much of it, as much as I hate to bring this up, is highly critical of some of your testing methods. They've called you, as despicable as the names seem, a *mad scientist, unhinged lunatic, Frankenstein incarnate.* I wanted to know how you and your office are handling this response from the populous?"

"Well, Ziles, I appreciate you bringing up this topic. This type of response is actually not at all new. Our procedures at The Laboratory have always been a source of some controversy. Nearly 10 years ago, there was a whole scandal about us performing trials that ended up being fatal for a group of school-aged children. Of course, this was ultimately discredited, and we won a hefty defamation lawsuit in lieu of those reports. But at the end of the day, our office is working day and night to bring healthy and sustainable solutions to the people of this great-"

Ari had heard enough of that man's pompous words and couldn't hold back anymore. She angrily swiped her open hand across the table, connecting with the speaker. His words seemed to fade as the radio flew across the room, and he shut up abruptly as chunks of metal and strings of wires flew in all directions. She stormed out the foyer and went to pull open the door. A screeching alarm blared as she rolled her eyes in anguish. She put her mask on and turned the knob again, stumbling out the door as it flew open, dust slowly floating up from beneath her feet. She rushed through the huge station, bustling with people trying to make it to the right train. She looked frantically until she saw a green train with an electronic sign with the words "Towards Red Rock Station" in bright yellow letters. She shoved past the endless hordes, sliding and juking her way towards the doors.

"Doors closing," a robotic woman's voice announced. She put her head down and almost ran over an old lady as she saw the mechanical doors start to close. "Doors closing," mocked her as she desperately sprinted. "Doors closing." She grinded her teeth below her mask. "Doors closing." She pumped her arms as fast as she could. "Doors closing."

She rushed through the double doors just as they shut, skipping the small gap between the train and the platform. As the door closed, a *swish* sound reverberated throughout the car, signifying an airtight seal. Everyone looked at her with contempt. She didn't care in the slightest.

"Warning, the train is about to depart. Please make sure you are seated, and all personal belongings are secured." Ari quickly found an open seat and placed the backpack in the bin on the seat in front of her. A few seconds passed, and the train instantly accelerated to its cruising pace. As they exited the train station, the world was an endless red mass around her.

She recognized the familiar terrain and prepared for departure. She reached into the bin in front of her to retrieve her bag, but it seemed to be stuck to the bottom. She pulled harder, and it wouldn't give. She peeked inside to see a spilled RAZORBURN energy drink coated throughout the bin. *Of fucking course, the perfect addition to my already glamorous day.* She refused to pull harder for the risk of tearing the delicate fabric.

She swallowed her pride and lowered a hesitant hand down into the bin. *This is some gross shit.* She carefully peeled the bottom of the bag away from the sticky substance, inch by grueling inch. Finally, she safely removed the precious cargo away from that mess. She cleaned her hands with a wipe that she retrieved from the bag but couldn't escape the gross feeling. At least the bag didn't rip.

"Final stop. Red Rock Station," exclaimed the robot woman.

Ari tipped an invisible cap towards the train speaker as she shuffled with the rest of the riders off the train. "Thank ya, ma'am!" she said, a morning ritual that gave her a little bit of sunshine in her mostly dark morning trek. Even though she was desensitized from going there five days a week for over 3 years, Red Rock Station was the most beautiful out of all the stations. The walls were almost completely glass, showing off the dunes scattered with giant red rocks of all sizes and shapes. The outside was like a blur on the train, but slowing to appreciate them made one realize the complexity of each inanimate piece of the red landscape. Mountain ranges slinked along in red streaks as far as the eye could see. Most had wide bases with narrow peaks poking off in any particular direction. Although some rose up like tidal waves, traveling miles into the air, penetrating the sky. Of course, this view is completely ruined by the giant apartment complex that seemed to loom over everything.

A Laboratory drone suddenly blasted past her head, a medicinal capsule attached to the underside of its frame. Flying up the side of the building, it entered one of the homes through the window. It quickly exited and dropped down to ground level, ready to fly by her again. As it drew closer, she suddenly threw up her arm, blocking its course. The robot banked left and into the ground. It shuddered slightly and attempted to fly, spinning out and colliding with the ground again. As its camera turned towards her, she gave the drone the one-finger salute. "Eat shit, doctor." She spun on her heel and continued to walk. There was probably a zero percent chance that he was going to see that, but just the action itself was empowering, and Ari could take any victory she could get these days.

She approached a silver building with rounded corners that

were built into a particularly massive rock. "Red Rocks Travel Co." was plastered in magenta letters in front. *Another day, another dollar.* Ari trudged up the hard metal steps, feeling the weight of each footfall. She entered the first set of doors, then the next, and was greeted with the warm, well-conditioned air of the office space.

She stood in front of the time tracker that would clock her in for the day. "Please stand still as retinal scans are performed." She stood still with a hand on each hip and her head lazily leaning to the side. "Identity confirmed, welcome Ari Matos." She walked over to the break room, pulling the now-squished sandwich out of her bag. The fridge was full when she opened the door, but she not so delicately shifted other people's items around to make room for her own. She turned from the fridge to see a scrawny man in his 30s. Gharrie was a decent-looking guy and was quite nice, but his nasally voice made Ari hope, respectfully, that he would never speak ever again.

"Another glorious morning! What. Is. Up. With. You. R. E," he said, pulling out and shooting her with his finger guns.

Ari groaned. She should have expected this overwhelming ray of sunshine would blind her on this disgusting, gloomy morning. She didn't necessarily hate Gharrie. However, she did not particularly enjoy morning people, which was a group that Gharrie unfortunately not only was a part of but ruled with an iron fist.

"I'm doing fine. I'm guessing your…"

"Splendid! You are correct, miss Doom n' Gloom."

Ari visibly shuttered. She has been working with Gharrie for 3 years. 3 whole years. And she still wasn't used to his antics. However, she felt bad for the guy. He was a happy little cog in the machine, a person who was fine with sitting down. Fine with mediocrity. But hey, who was the happy one?

Gharrie, obviously allergic to awkward silences, switched gears: "You hear about that new drug The Laboratory…"

"Gharrie," Ari interrupted with a deadly hiss and an even deadlier stare. "You know that…"

"I *know*. I *know*," Gharrie threw his hands in the air, "I know you hate when I talk about the Laboratory." Gharrie squinted at her quizzically, "I won't ask you why you hate The Laboratory so much…" Ari shrunk inside herself. She watched his eyes, for the first time ever, start to darken from the usual bright blue.

"I have known you for a little while Ari, and you don't really open up much. But words aren't always needed to tell a story. You hate when I mention The Laboratory, so I had a strong feeling that you are the rebel type. Someone who wants down with authority and wants to stick it to 'The Man.' Let me tell you a story. I was on my way to work, just on my merry way, when I see one of those drones delivering those new happy pills I was gonna tell you about. Now, this is the good part. I see this drone drop off those pills in someone's house. When it comes back down, I see it crash in the middle of Red Rock Station. Some woman threw it off course. Must have been an accident. *Surely* no one would go out of their way to knock a drug drone to the ground…hold on a second! The woman walks over to this drone and *flips it off!* Seriously. I have never seen anyone do something so asinine in my life. Now, I wonder who that woman was."

Gharrie looks at the backpack and back at Ari, who looks away, blushing. "And I wonder what that woman was thinking. A drug drone? Seriously? What did that really accomplish? Big deal. She must have felt so good sticking it to the big bad Laboratory. Now let me ask you a question, Ari. How many people order drugs from the Laboratory? How many drones do you think they have made to accommodate those people? How many repairmen are there to repair those drones that took a little tumble?" Gharrie's eyes softened for a second, and he looked down at his boots. "That woman's feelings are more widespread than she thinks. She is definitely not alone. There were other people who were affected by what The Laboratory has done. Not everyone is as stupid as you think they are."

A stunned silence lay heavy in the air.

"I hope, though," Gharrie continued, "That woman realizes that some mountains are too treacherous to climb. Sometimes the hero doesn't get the princess. Sometimes the little guy loses, and there is nothing he can do. No revenge story. No vindication. Maybe she should just give up like the rest of us did a long time ago."

Gharrie pulled out a little capsule and swallowed it. His eyes turned back to their normal shade of blue. His lips curled into an unusually large smile. "Now. It is time to show off this beautiful world we live in to some lucky people!" He turned and left the breakroom.

Ari didn't know what to say. She was slack-jawed, staring at Gharrie, the man she thought she knew these past couple years, who walked away like nothing happened. *What the fuck just happened? Who the fuck is Gharrie? What were those pills?* She looked at the clock. *We will unpack that later I guess.* She strutted quickly over to the front desk.

"What does my schedule look like today, Mauro?" Ari asked, leaning over the granite counter where a dark-haired, clean-shaven man sat attentively in a swivel chair.

"You've got a premium tour starting in oh about," he took a glance at his watch, "three minutes. Sorry for the late notice. Then a standard tour after lunch, and you'll be ending the day with the whole shebang, the full circle around Red Rocks."

"Damn."

"Yeah, well, at least you'll get overtime," Mauro said with a wink. "We can all use that. You better get out back. The tour group is already waiting. And just so you know, they are on the more entitled side of things.

"Okay, thanks Mauro. See you later."

Another day showing these fucking yuppies some big red rocks. Hooray for me.

She walked towards the back of the building, finding an assortment of electronic fobs hooked to a cork board. She grabbed number 4 off the shelf and exited the secured back door, the doors screeching as they reluctantly opened. She was excited to see seven figures huddled around the Roamer 3000. A short woman holding a baby with a pink mask speckled with glitter seemed to have asserted herself as the leader of the group. She stepped forward to meet Ari.

"Excuse me, we've been waiting for nearly 10 minutes already. If I would've known that the Travel Co. had such little respect for their customers-"

"Sorry for the delay ma'am," Ari said.

You should just have bitch plastered on your forehead if you're going to be that obvious about it.

"I was just figuring out some of the logistics of the tour. It is very nice to meet everyone, my name is Ari, and I will be your tour guide for today. I have the pleasure of showing you all around the lower gorge area of Red Rocks today. Let's get goin', shall we?"

"Finally," grumbled a pudgy-looking tourist as they all climbed into the Roamer.

Hot crowd, hot crowd. As she started to pull away from the charging station, she pointed to a large collection of spikes rising thousands of feet in elevation. "If you look over to this mountain range in the distance…" She looked back to see half of the people staring at their arm bands, their fingers scrolling aimlessly on their smudged screens. Ari's eyes twitched. *Another group of ungrateful shits that our government has manufactured through their encouraging overindulgence in those candy-flavored pills. They would tie their shoelaces together and put their masks on backward if their cherished Dr. Thominson told them to..*

"In. The. Distance!" Ari's voice rose to a roar as everyone perked up in surprise. *You listening now, you disgraceful oafs?* She smiled inwardly for a second before continuing her spiel. "You can see this huge volcano that towers over everything. This is the largest volcano known to man right now." She looked down at a little boy holding his mother's hand in the front seat, his rust colored mask huge on his tiny body. He was mesmerized by the rocky behemoth as it swam with the stars in his eyes. Those curious eyes...

She shook her head and focused back on the road. This part was going to be difficult to navigate. She drove the Roamer down a slope and into the entrance of a narrow box canyon. The walls felt as if they were squeezing the air out of the vehicle. She navigated the vehicle carefully through this section, not exceeding a crawling pace. The ride became bumpy as Ari rode over rocks that had crumbled away from the canyon and gathered on the floor below. She could hear the innocent boy behind her gasp as she rode over a particularly large rock. She swiveled around in her pilot's seat to make sure he was okay; what a poor thing.

Finally, the walls of the godforsaken canyon began to shrink, and she sped down the rocky slope that led out to the exit. As they emerged, she could feel the tourist's mouths drop open and lungs empty as the city emerged into view. She had seen the look many times before, utter amazement at the modern city skyline featured in front of a vast wasteland of red dust with ageless mountains in the distance.

"Wow, kids, take a look at that. Look at your new town from up here. All your friends back home sure would be jealous." The pink masked woman stated.

I'm sure they wouldn't be jealous you had to have a hunk of metal strapped to your face whenever you stepped outside and swallowed the pills mommy gave you like a good little boy.

"I've never seen anything quite like it," a man with the voice of an eccentric college professor said. "Quite an extraordinary view."

"Indeed, a true miracle of modern engineering." The man beside him stated.

Digging up natural rocks and replacing them with characterless, bland modern structures. What a miracle.

Ari pulled the vehicle around a boulder, partially obstructing the view, and then came to a halt.

"You folks can step outside of the vehicle to get a better view and take some pictures if you'd like. I will be here to answer any questions you might have." The guests slowly exited and stretched their legs.

"Wow... that one is truly fascinating-" the professor said, pointing in the general direction of a bullet-like structure rising above the rest of the skyline. Its outer surface was translucent glass, tinted with amber. Near the top, it began to spiral, twisting in on itself until the culmination at where there was a striking red light display advertising the newest product from The Laboratory. Ari imagined some ritual sacrifice was performed at the top of the structure, above the digital advertisement unit. Above the countless citizens unaware of the corporate greed and malevolence.

"That is *The Laboratory* headquarters."

"Impressive place… I sure would love an office up there," said the professor.

"I wouldn't. Dr. Thominson has an indescribable amount of pressure carrying the weight of our treasured city on his back," said the pretentious pink masked woman. "Think of how we all rely on him for the Omni pills and our precious protection from the toxic air," She was interrupted by the sound of crying from her lap as her baby started to wail. She absentmindedly took out a pill bottle and inserted the pill into the baby's feeding tube. "What would we do without him?"

How hard his job must be true, brainwashing a population of small-minded drug addicts. Feeding a fucking infant happy pills. What planet am I on?

"A fair point indeed, ma'am, I never thought about it quite like that," said the professor.

"Regardless, he must have a spectacular view up there in *Laboratory Tower*," said the man next to him.

A spectacular view that was earned by illegal drug testing and the manufacturing of a drug that allowed him to control the city and its people. Not to mention the fearmongering of a population to wear masks constantly to prevent an airborne illness we're not even sure exists. What a rightful fortune he's earned. What a just and honest man he is.

"There's a lot more to see over in this direction." Ari motioned the guests away from the obsession with the greedy man's tower. "You can see the central station to the east, the convergence of all the high-speed rails in the valley. Just take a look to the right of the tower. It's the round glass dome."

"Ultimately, I don't think The Laboratory gets the respect they deserve." The professor ignored Ari and continued the unsettling topic of conversation. "They single-handedly saved a population from its own destruction. They gave us the pills to virtually solve mental illness and increase our productivity. They gave us breath and the prevention of the most toxic airborne disease known to man. Where would we be without them?"

We would be independent, creative, self-sufficient, and most importantly: not fucking puppets in a billionaires playhouse.

Ari looked down at the little boy with the sweet eyes that had found his way back to his mother after jumping between rocks. What an innocent kid. He hasn't seen the true shit this world can throw at you yet, and she hoped he wouldn't have to anytime soon.

"Exactly, think of where we *wouldn't* be if not for everything The Laboratory has done. And especially the new direction the organization has gone in with the help of Dr. Thominson."

Great, another line of company bullshit propaganda.

"I mean, think of all the improvements he's made to the Omni pills and mask design. A true genius. And it seems like a product of all the testing he's done recently."

"Oh yes, I've heard they are looking for young children to participate in the new batch of clinical trials. It comes with hefty compensation. And a chance to make history, of course." The professor's companion said.

You'd be a fucking fool to take that deal.

"Wow! What a treat that would be." She looked down at her little boy, his Rust colored mask dotted with little stickers. He was playing with the sand at his mother's feet.

Don't you fucking dare bitch.

"I'll check it out when I get home. We would love to have Ollie take part. What an honor! He will surely thank us when he's older. My little boy could make history." She took Ollie into her arms, hugging him tightly. "The good doctor will take care of you, sweetie."

Ari's hands shook violently as her fingers closed into tight fists. Black clouds filled her eyes as tears started to stream down her cheeks. *You won, Doctor. You won.* Calmly she turned on her heel and began to walk away.

As she drifted farther from the tour group, she looked towards the deep, black sky riddled with shiny stars that looked down on her like tiny angels. She liked to think that Leo was watching her as some sort of star cluster, nebula, or supernova, waving from light years above.

She couldn't hear the confused and surprised calls of the tourists, watching their tour guide stride away. She slowly turned the knob on the back of her head and could feel a slight amount of pressure release along with a hissing sound that accompanied it. Her hand hovered for a moment over the small button on the left side of her head that controlled the front mask over her face. Her fingers twitched. Hours passed in the span of seconds. Time became a matter of stretched-out moments, moments that will never happen again and go on forever. For the first time, she was in control. She pressed the button.

Her mask screeched open, and she immediately felt the frigidity of space. Her last breath of oxygen fizzled out in the cold, unforgiving air. Choking, she felt the stillness of space flow through her. Her eyes drove towards a dark tunnel as black slowly constricted her vision. The world around her seemed to fade away as she fell into the void. Her body collapsed, becoming one with the red sand below her. The last view she had was the stars undisturbed, shining brightly down upon the rugged face of Mars. Leo was smiling.

AUTHOR BIOS

Jon Richter writes dark fiction, and is the author of four crime thrillers (Chains, Rabbit Hole, Never Rest and Deadly Burial) as well as two collections of short horror fiction (Jon Richter's Disturbing Works, Volumes One and Two), cyberpunk thriller Auxiliary, and psychological techno-thriller The Warden.

Jon lives in London and spends some of his time hiding in the guise of his sinister alter ego, an accountant called Dave. When he isn't counting beans, he is a self-confessed nerd who loves books, films and video games – basically any way to tell a great story!

If you want to chat to him about this, or about anything at all, you can find him on Twitter @RichterWrites or Instagram @jonrichterwrites; he'd also love it if you would check out his website at www.jon-richter.com. Jon also co-hosts two podcasts: the dark fiction podcast, Dark Natter, and the cyberpunk podcast, Hosts In The Shell, which you can find wherever you get your podcast fix.

Titania Tempest is a lifelong reader and some-time writer of Fantasy and Sci-Fi. She was heavily inspired from a young age by the myriad works of Anne McCaffrey, and in particular the Crystal Singer Series and Chronicles of Pern.

Titania writes mostly high fantasy, and her works also regularly feature sapphic themes. As a sapphic herself, her dream is to give others the heroines she thirsted for whilst growing up.

Titania's future goal is to publish her two Works-In-Progress: "Shadowblood", a sapphic Dark Fantasy novel set in the fictional world of Andoherra, and "Dawn & Rosie", a Comedy Romance that explores the relationship between two women in their early sixties. Dawn (widowed) and Rosie (divorced)—fast friends, tentative lovers, and all-around hilarious individuals—are thrown together in a sort of British-Sitcom-feel story with a happy ending.

Steve DeGroof is an expat Canadian who now lives in North Carolina. He has worked, at one time or other, as: a TV repairman, a security guard at a children's hospital, and a janitor in a strip club. His current day job is as a software developer for a regional bank, which is considerably less dangerous and messy.

He honed his writing skills publishing the webcomic "Tree Lobsters" and screenwriting for the YouTube series "Death by Puppets". When not busy refining his art, such as a clock in the shape of Rick Astley that chimes "Never Gonna Give You Up" on the hour (for which he is sincerely sorry), he published six collections of short stories and two novels, with no plans of stopping any time soon.

Alex O'Neal (*Homo sapiens nerdii*) can be seen in the wild near books or technology, solving problems with either design or writing (fiction, non-fiction, and poetry). She is a late-diagnosed autistic woman who doesn't care what pronoun you call her and is incomplete without a dog. Alex's autism-level obsessions include taxonomy, color, dogs, Tolkien, and making information more usable, but she's also vocal about disability rights and helped found a disability resource group at a major tech company. Although she has had an award-winning tech career (as well as many non-tech jobs), she finds herself writing more and more.

Alex has been spotted in various locations in North America, South America, and Europe, but current resides in the Texas Hill Country with her neurodivergent mate, a particularly smart example of *Canis lupus familiaris*, two *Felis cati**, and whatever other creatures happen by.

*Plural of *catus*.

Jeanne Franc, a retired educator, loves creating intricate fantasy worlds and bringing to life the unknown backstories of fairy-tale characters. She has written several novels and many short stories; TRICKERY is her first official published work. She is currently working on a dark fantasy set in the portal worlds of Bleak City and Auld Wirld.

When not writing, or thinking about writing, she is an avid reader of mysteries and science, an enthusiastic baseball fan, and a winter escapee to Portugal. She and her husband live in a quiet part of southwestern Ontario, Canada and are 'parents' to a fussy senior feline who truly believes he is helping when he sits on the computer.

Jim Kiernan is a military science fiction author, gamer, musician, husband, son, brother, and many other things. He often says that his biggest problem in life is that he wants to try everything, but has prioritized literature, gaming, and the outdoors. He lives in the hills of the New York Capital Region with his wife, and three eccentric cats. There may also be a feral cat who roams his property, defending it from the marauding hordes in exchange for food and a comfy shed. You can find Jim on Twitter and Instagram, where he would love to connect with his readers!

Josh Spicer is a young writer from the North Shore in Massachusetts. He loves short story writing, but he does indulge in writing poetry from time to time. He has a collection of poems under a pen name and has poems featured in Outrageous Fortune Magazine. Some day he hopes to be a full time writer and poet.

Kia Jones is an independent author, offering both her fictional stories and personal life experiences through Patreon. All of her works are heavily women dominated, and typically offer a unique twist on common knowledge/occurrences. 'In The Town of Ambermoure' was heavily inspired by the decision made in the Supreme Court back in June 2022, but she wanted to offer a...strange twist to it. In all of the pieces you can access on her Patreon, a similar theme is heavily present; women who break a standard, who are loud, take up space, make mistakes, and do hard things. Growing up, the message she needed to hear most was that being a woman didn't have to be a hindrance. Being a woman meant being powerful, headstrong and, most importantly, human. She needed those stories, so she wrote those stories; for herself, and for others.

'In The Town of Ambermoure' gives you a little glimpse of that, and she is absolutely thrilled to be partnering with Strangest Fiction to bring you this story.

Find her Patreon at Patreon.com/alifeofvalor

Stephen Faulkner is a native New Yorker who was transplanted with his wife, Joyce, to Atlanta, Georgia. They are now both retired and living the good life in Central Florida, keeping busy volunteering at different non-profit organizations and going to the theater as often as they can find the time. He has recently had stories published in such publications as Aphelion Webzine, Hellfire Crossroads, Temptation Magazine, The Erotic Review, Liquid Imagination, Sanitarium Magazine, The Satirist, Foliate Oak Literary Magazine, Fictive Dream, Flash Fiction Magazine, The Literary Hatchet, ZiN Daily and AHF (Alternative History Fiction) Magazine. His novel, Aliana in Paradise was published by World Castle Publishing in November, 2018 and is available through Amazon.com and Barnesandnoble.com. His second novel, Lunar Effects was published by Eden Stories in September, 2020. Speculations, a book of short stories, has just been released by Bridge House Publishing in November, 2021.

Alex Mann has always taken the hard road and followed his dreams. With his words he creates worlds that he wants to read about and now he brings that same passion to the world. Growing up watching the fantasy movies of the 80s, and 90s he brings that over-the-top adventure tempered by the furnace of emotional exploration. He lives in the mountains of Montana using inspiration from nature to build a more vibrant world to explore through writing. When not writing he enjoys taking care of his one-winged pigeon "Gerald" and Pitbull "Daisy", cooking and relaxing with his spouse. If nothing else, he wants his work to inspire others to follow their dreams no matter where they may lead.

Micheal Onofrio was born and raised in Wichita, Kansas. As of right now, after switching majors and career paths, he has landed on Secondary Education in English as a major while attending Kansas State University. He grew up watching Scooby Doo and eventually landed on horror movies as his favorite source of entertainment, which informs and inspires the short stories that he writes today. His hope for the future is that he becomes a successful English teacher and writes for fun on the side.

E.L. McKenzie recently relocated to the East Village in Manhattan, leaving the beauty and serenity of Colorado's mountains for the hustle and bustle of New York City. He spends his days quietly writing and observing life from his second avenue apartment. Nights are for enjoying the artsy eclectic experiences readily available. He is currently working on his third novel in the Nick Lynch crime thriller series.

William Merrill lives in the panhandle of Florida and absolutely loves it there less the hurricanes, and floods, and heat, and humidity, and tourist drivers and the bugs. If 50 is the new 40, he is 41 years old. He has a

Wife, three kids and a bona fide job. The ice-cream truck comes through his neighborhood about twice a week. His parents were pretty much hippies with English degrees and they both loved writing and talking about writing. He couldn't understand it because their passion made him anything but wealthy. By the age of 17, he hated the thought of anything to do with writing so much that he rebelled and became an engineer. He sure as shit showed them. He wrote 'Decapitator 2.0' shortly after two of his family members died, both of cancer...slowly and painfully. Not long after they passed, his son and him were at an amusement park riding a roller coaster when the train ducked under a metal girder that gave the illusion it was going to decapitate everyone. After he stopped squeezing the seat between my cheeks, a thought occurred to him; why is it that we think a sudden, violent, gruesome, but mostly painless death is a much worse way to leave this world than a slow, painful, bedriddien death? In his own Strangest Fiction way, he wrote this piece as part of his grieving and as his way to answer that question.

Derek Wautlet is the founder of strangestfiction.com and Strangest Fiction, LLC. He started the site in order to create a safe haven for emerging authors to explore their passion for "strange" and experimental fiction writing without any restrictions. He is a Wisconsin native that loves the great outdoors and the serenity of writing in hipster coffee shops. In the future he hopes to continue growing the Strangest Fiction community to increase the value it can bring to its authors! You can find out more about him and all his endeavors at derekwautlet.com.

Darrell Grant is a retired New York City Police Officer who started writing short stories a couple of years ago, whenever they came to mind. Darrell loves reading and writing in all genres except romance but luckily for Darrell, his wife who he wrote this story for, knows that he is deeply in love with her. Fantasy, Mysteries, Sci-Fi and Thrillers are what he likes the most. To me there is nothing like writing a story that someone else can enjoy, imagine and visualize as they read . He hopes this short story of "The Book Of Books " enables you to do just that.

Henry Valerio (Henry Vinicio Valerio Madriz) was born in Atenas, Costa Rica in 1969. The author is a teacher who studied and graduated in English Teaching and Linguistics and Literature. He also enjoys drawing and painting and outdoor activities. He has taught English and Spanish (also in the USA), as foreign languages, for almost 30 years; he is currently working for the Ministry of Public Education, at a bilingual public high school, in San Carlos, Costa Rica. He is also the author of "Strange Fate", a short story in Darkness Falls (anthology), The Red Penguin Collection.

Will Hershey is well traveled, having lived in places like Massachusetts, Wisconsin, London, and Prague. Nowadays, Will owns a small literary themed coffee shop in the countryside of New England. When he's not running his humble establishment, he is conjuring up stories, stargazing, and curling up with a creepy book. He has dreams of becoming a famous writer one day and he hopes that "Miss Doom N' Gloom" will be a good start towards that goal.

STRANGEST FICTION ANTHOLOGIES
Fascinating Short Fiction Stories

More anthologies are coming soon! Please be on the lookout. Post a story for free consideration anytime at strangestfiction.com.

Made in United States
Cleveland, OH
03 May 2025

16622890R00144